The Art of Being One

To Evie
Thank you for reading my books!
Best Wishes.
Malcolm

The Art of Being One

Malcolm McClean

bearhunt

Copyright © 2015 Malcolm McClean

The right of Malcolm McClean to be identified as the Author of the work has been asserted by him in accordance with the Copyright, Design and Patents Act 1988

First published in 2015
By BEARHUNT

Apart from any use permitted under UK copyright law, this publication may only be reproduced, stored or transmitted, in any form, or by any means, with prior permission in writing of the publishers or, in the case of reprographic production, in accordance with the terms of licences issued by the Copyright Licensing Agency.

This book is a work of fiction. Names, characters, places and incidents either are a product of the author's imagination or are used fictitiously, and any resemblance to actual persons living or dead, events or locales is entirely coincidental.

Every effort has been made to fulfil requirements with regard to reproducing copyright material. The author and publisher will be glad to rectify any omissions at the earliest opportunity.

Cataloguing in Publication Data is available from the British Library

Paperback ISBN 978-0-9931986-0-1
eBook ISBN 978-0-9931986-1-8

I'm Forever Blowing Bubbles: Words and music by John Kellette & Jaan Kenbrovin
Klunkaren/Neri Nesets Minne: Halvard T Bjørgum
Slinkombas: Halvard T Bjørgum
Bjorgumspel: Torliev H Bjørgum

Typeset by Palimpsest Book Production Limited, Falkirk, Stirlingshire

Printed and bound in Great Britain by
Clays, St Ives plc

BEARHUNT
St Hilary's Park
Alderley Edge SK9 7DA

www.bearhunt.org.uk

To Joyce
Thank you for the maps

CHAPTER ONE
THE BUBBLE

It started with a bubble.

Nobody's quite sure when it happened, but it seemed that suddenly people began living in 'bubbles'.

Maybe it was when political hacks began obsessing about the 'Westminster Bubble'; or when the only thing that mattered to breakfast TV presenters was the 'Hollywood Bubble'.

All anyone really knows is that, one day, some dullard sports journalist thought that he would jump on the bandwagon. He created 'The Premiership Bubble', a cotton wool world inhabited, or so the public were led to believe, by overpaid, underworked, egotistical, shallow and spoilt professional footballers.

This was Jonathan Christie's world. A goalkeeper by trade, the one-time last line of defence for one-time Champions of

Europe. Even he would have to admit there were some truths in the media generalisations. Of course there were. But for this particular 'Number One', this world was beginning to suffocate and choke. Slowly crushing the life and soul out of him.

It was the small things at first. Like the time he tried to start an actual conversation. Take some interest in the outside world, by raising the topic of 'The Arab Spring' at a pre-match meal in a hotel just outside Newcastle.

There was an awkward silence and a few anxious glances across the table until someone did what they always did when they were unsure of themselves. Talk bollocks.

"Yeah, The Arab Spring. I won the school high jump with that. Much better than The Fosbury Flop."

The bubble with the lifestyle 'to die for' was under constant scrutiny, sometimes to the point of obsession. Yet the truth is that if you could have looked closely enough into their world you might have been surprised. Disappointed even. On closer inspection, interesting became mundane with a capital 'M'.

To say so at the time would have been heresy. Moaning about being locked in a gilded cage on an average wage of fifty-seven grand a week just doesn't go down well with the public. Yet the more it went on, the more Christie found himself fronting an ever decaying façade; appearing to be successful on the outside, yet slowly dying on the inside.

He thought about this sometimes. Wondered what life might be like on the 'outside' as if he were a lifer in a gold-plated seven star prison designed by an oil rich sheik.

But the outside world seemed a foreign place. A place

THE ART OF BEING ONE

inhabited by normal people who did normal things. They didn't even pay the wages anymore, the TV moguls did that.

He and the others just put it out of their minds. Goalkeepers are good at that. When you stand in front of seventy-thousand screaming fans for a living, you just have to be able to tune them out. Christie always did.

Until that one day. Playing away at West Ham. He began to notice the sound of the crowd seeping into his mind. Slowly at first. Like the hum of an approaching army some way in the distance. Then rising as if a swarm of killer bees was about to enter through the players tunnel until the drone turned into a melody in the way that a long forgotten radio station emerges from the static. The crowd were singing.

> "I'm forever blowing bubbles
> Pretty bubbles in the air
> They fly so high, nearly reach the sky
> Like Jonathan Christie they fade and die."

The Number One seemed lost, staring at the sky and drifting outside of his penalty area towards the tunnel.

Then something in his head seemed to go 'pop'.

The bubble had burst.

CHAPTER TWO
JUST ONE

For as long as he could remember, people had always described Jonathan Christie as 'different', even a little strange. A loner. A kid who liked his own space. He didn't see it like that of course. He just did what came natural to him. A boy who was happy with his thoughts. The type who lived in his imagination. Pondering random maps that his mum pulled out of litter bins in the tower block of offices that she cleaned before breakfast and after dinner, arriving home to the theme tune of Coronation Street.

He would sit quietly, hoping that as she unpacked her bag, tonight would be one of those nights when she had found some tattered outline of the former Yugoslavia or a redundant touristic pamphlet of the Iberian Peninsula.

In reality, this rarely happened, but such was the escape from the mundane brought about by routes, contours and imagination, by 7.30pm he was always in a heightened state of alert.

He was happy to sit and stare at his crumpled maps, sometimes for hours on end, occasionally whispering quietly the names of strange sounding places. He particularly liked Saskatchewan and Reykjavik. They were his favourites really, and he would try to imagine what life could possibly be like in these far-flung regions that his mum had rescued from the incinerator.

She knew that he had a special talent when at the age of two she had tossed a tennis ball in his direction, thinking that he would give chase and toss it back. He caught it instantly before throwing it back in her direction. Surprised, smiling, she returned the compliment, first to the left then to the right, then a high one. Each time he kept his head in the same place, looking straight ahead, catching the ball using a combination of instinct and peripheral vision.

After that he was rarely seen without a ball in his hands or at his feet, inventing games with ever more complex rules and scoring methods. He kept tallies in an old exercise book, and just like a kid obsessed with acting, he played all of the parts. He was the home team one moment and the away team the next, priding himself on his fairness and impartiality and enjoying the calculations as he re-jigged his league tables after each of his imaginary fixtures.

Nobody ever spoke about his dad. He had enquired but there was never an explanation.

"It's just us son. Just us" his mum would say before busying herself trying to remove an imaginary stain from a worktop or rearranging a couple of tins of Heinz Mulligatawny.

He liked to imagine that his dad had moved to Saskatchewen

and that one day an envelope would arrive with an aeroplane ticket and a note that just said 'meet me at Calgary airport'. In the back of his exercise book he kept a crumpled piece of tracing paper where in soft pencil he had tracked the route from Calgary to Saskatchewen. Just in case.

He was just thirteen when it happened. It was no longer 'Just us'. He had noticed that his mum had lost weight, but it was not something they talked about. They spoke when something needed to be said. It was not really for him to get into the ins and outs of women's weight issues. She'd taken on extra work during the day to pay for the goalkeeping gloves, the boots that he grew out of on a regular basis and to feed the appetite of a lad that looked like he would not stop growing. Three jobs was the equivalent of a serious workout every day. She was bound to shed a few pounds.

When a few pounds became a couple of stone, he'd look at her expecting her to tell him that everything was going to be all right, but they never talked of feelings or emotions or even of the future. Those things were for people who lived in proper families. He longed to tell her all about their new life in Saskatchewen. He was sure that dad would send two tickets. They would live in a log cabin and hunt bear. She'd be sure to put on weight. But he never did mention it.

Even at thirteen he had a pre-match routine. Zoning himself out so that the horseplay, the wedgies and the Chinese burns that were the stock-in-trade of the school first team, seemed like the gentle hum of a Calgary bound 747 as he stared straight ahead using coat peg number seventeen as a focal point for his gaze.

Bignose, the overbearing military style PE teacher cast a

shadow over coat peg number seventeen, but for once he wasn't fizzing with his irrepressible enthusiasm.

"Christie, you'll need to let Murray have the Number One shirt" he said.

Jonathan politely protested. He'd seen his name on the teamsheet, he was always number one.

"I'll need to see you outside" said Bignose as if he was about to announce the death of another member of the armed forces in Afghanistan.

"Just us" was now "Just one."

That was the beginning of the art of being one.

It was sporting history in a way. It was normal for players to leave the pitch if they were injured, or to get substituted, but as far as anyone could remember, Jonathan Christie was the first professional player in history to walk off with the game still in progress.

The press pack that had gathered for the post match interview was in a state of frenzy. It was as if a football crowd had decamped from the terraces to the media suite. They were as excited as any press pack had ever been. As for the game, well that had been a mundane affair, but this incident had provided the talking point that they hoped would fill some extra column inches. All they needed now was for Christie to be put before them like a lamb to the slaughter.

There was a collective groan of disappointment when the

manager, Roberto Capriolo appeared behind a bank of microphones, tilted his head and ran his fingers through his shaggy grey mane. His Italian accent fired his words staccato across the heads of the crowd, like a response of small arms fire.

"We talk about the game" he said "That's all."

"But Roberto, is it true that you and Christie traded punches at half time?" enquired an obese hack.

"Brian, you make this thing up. Jonathan, he is gentleman. I don't know why he do this thing. That's all. Ask me about the game."

In the front row, a slender brunette gently closed her laptop and caught the gaze of Capriolo.

"Mr Capriolo, you must understand that we are all very concerned about Christie. Do you think he might be depressed?"

Capriolo feigned exasperation "Tell me, how can you be depressed on fifty-seven grand a week? Now I say once again, we talk about the game."

Obligingly there were a series of standard questions about formation, tactics and then one last counter attack.

"Will Christie be suspended for this? Will you sack him?"

"We deal with this internally. We talk with Jonathan. Right now, we have no idea where he is."

Capriolo stood up sharply and turned on his heel to be ushered through a side door by a security man and a PR, as an avalanche of questions roared in his direction. None was able to stop him in his tracks.

There were inevitable stares as Jonathan made his way through the streets of East London from the Boleyn Ground and along Green Street. A grown man in full football kit, striding through the early spring sunshine past the market stalls selling yams and white sports socks. He looked like a man on a mission. Staring straight ahead as if zoning out on coat peg number seventeen, but in truth he had no idea where he was going. No idea what this might mean. He just knew one thing. He had to get away from this place.

A stallholder twirling a brown paper bag containing tomatoes was shouting repeatedly.

"Parnd a mush feeeefty peeee" before spotting Jonathan and trailing off mid sentence "Parnd a . . . ere, geezer you're going the wrong way, the football ground's back there . . ." Then turning to his small queue of customers and orchestrating a collective cackle of laughter.

Jonathan may have received more taunts before he reached Upton Park tube station, but if he did he was unaware of them. His pace quickened so that the plastic blades of his football boots began to slip as if the pavement had suddenly become covered with a sheet of ice.

Upton Park station was a foreign place as far as Jonathan was concerned. Any tube station would have been. He just didn't get it, any of it. The barriers, the ticket machines, the swarms of people who all made everything look so simple. He had never had to get it. It was probably twelve or thirteen years ago that he had last been on any form of public transport and that was the bus from his digs in Manchester when he was a youth team player. Tube trains. They were something else.

He stood motionless for a while watching people ebb and

flow through the turnstiles. Two guards stood by the barriers and eyed him suspiciously so, nervously, he picked up a leaflet from a rack, unfolded it and began to survey the map of the London Underground system.

There was something strangely comforting in the geometry. The clean lines, the colour coded key, the names of the stations all somehow took him to a place where he felt at ease, and for a moment he was a child lost in his world of maps.

His eyes ran westbound along the central line before making a jolt along the Northern line then flitting to lines south of the river and then back up again. Every so often he came across the name of a station that intrigued him for whatever reason and he whispered its name to see how it sounded. Gunnersbury; Shepherds Bush Market; Harrow-on-the-Hill; Charing Cross; Gospel Oak.

A shaven headed ticket collector with an earpiece wired to a small transistor radio buried in his pocket, watched open mouthed for a while and then walked over to his two colleagues by the barrier. There was a discussion with the shaven headed one pointing to his earpiece and gesticulating, turning and pointing towards Jonathan. He stared hard, then turning back to the others wagged his thumb over his shoulder whilst vigorously nodding his head.

By now Jonathan was marvelling in the never-ending delight of the Circle line. Mansion House; Cannon Street; Monument; Tower Hill; Aldgate.

He pursed his lips as he prepared to quietly whisper the name "Aldgate" only to be jolted as if being awoken from a dream.

"Ere, you're the keeper that's done one, aren't you?"

It was the shaven headed one with the earpiece.

CHAPTER THREE
THE CHASE

Like a lot of Premier League managers, Roberto Capriolo had little time for the irritating newspaper hack that he referred to as 'The obese one'. His name was Brian Dugdale and like most sports reporters, he had once fancied himself as a bit of a player. He liked to think that he was 'the one that got away'. A rough diamond that passed under the radar screen of all the talent scouts from the big clubs.

In truth, he went unnoticed by the small clubs, the semi-professional clubs and, for that matter, the top two tiers of The Brian's Fry Inn Manchester Wednesday League. His finest hour coming in the 1982/83 season when his team Pressmans FC had finished third division runners-up, just a point behind Strangeways Prison, who for obvious reasons had to play all of their games at home.

The cheap plastic runners-up trophy that was his sole

honour from a short career as an amateur clogger, sat on a small shelf inside his work cubicle. The gold paint on the plastic statuette of a footballer, with a ball stuck to his foot, had cracked to reveal small spots of white plastic as if the player had at some time been peppered with gunfire.

Below 'the trophy cabinet' as he called it, was a scene of devastation in the form of a desk which lay somewhere underneath a mound of papers scattered randomly so as to cover virtually every speck of the light oak laminate. Dugdale struggled to clear a space with his elbow as he balanced a six-pack of Stella Artois in one hand and a formidable parcel of fish and chips in the other.

He cracked open a can and tore the paper from around his mound of food. Throwing a chip into his mouth, he licked his fingers and slammed half a dozen keystrokes on his computer keyboard to bring up the copy that he had emailed in earlier that day.

"Hammers draw blank as Christie does runner."

He tutted and shook his head whilst loading up his plastic fork and bowing to stuff the precariously balanced contents into his mouth. "Rubbish" he grunted still in the full throes of mastication. He could never understand why he wasn't allowed to write his own headlines. He leaned forwards to peer over the cubicle partition to try to catch sight of 'the kid' that they paid to come up with so called killer headlines.

With deadlines approaching everybody seemed too engrossed in their own stories to hear his complaints, even if they were interested. But it had been a long time since anyone in the office had been that interested in Dugdale's opinions. He was increasingly seen as an irritant. A relic from the past, seeing out his time, which for many in the neighbouring workstations, couldn't come soon enough.

Sleeping on the cubicle floor was not easy for a man of his size. His gut had been expanding steadily for some years now. Sitting down for a living; long nights and long drives home; service station food; his liking for real ale; none of it really helped. Yet the 59 year old had promised himself he'd get in shape for his retirement — if 'this' and but for 'that'.

There were a lot of ifs and buts in the life of Brian Dugdale. If he could get his head down in the cubicle without being noticed. If he could wake up before the boss got in.

But he couldn't. He awoke to small splashes of water being poured from a conical cup onto his forehead.

"Brian. My office." It was the boss.

Dugdale pushed open the glass door of the editor's office, slightly breathless and crumpled. A piece of his hair had matted and stuck out at 90 degrees from his head. This was more than just the 'lived-in' look, it was as if a bunch of squatters had taken possession and gone on a wrecking spree.

He squeezed into a tight leather chair and waited. Merlin Shoesmith finally turned from the plate glass window.

"For Christ's sake Brian. This isn't a hostel. How many times?"

"Sorry Chief. It's just, you know . . . I'm not seeing eye to eye with the missus."

"We've been through it before Brian. Don't eat that shit that you eat in the office. I've told you about the alcohol policy — this isn't bloody Fleet Street, and we're not the

Salvation Army either. This is the last time. Oh and I've told you to stop calling me Chief."

"Sorry Chief, It's just that's what we've always done. You know, called the Chief the Chief."

Shoesmith placed his head close to Dugdale's and whispered slowly for effect.

"Well we don't do it anymore. Get me? And while you're here Brian, you can't go on churning out these bland match reports. Yesterday's was dull, dull, dull."

Dugdale took issue with this. It was a dull nil-nil draw. The raw material wasn't great. He'd covered hundreds of matches in his career. Big ones too. Long listed for the Sports Writer of the Year 1989. He'd shown promise, even occasional panache.

"Take it up with the kid. That headline dull" he countered.

"No Brian. The only thing of interest that happened yesterday was Christie doing a runner. You mentioned it in the last paragraph. The last para? What were you thinking? The 'kid' as you put it, got it up front."

Merlin Shoesmith and the corporate culture had sort of crept up on Dugdale whilst he was busy 'taking one for the team' in rickety press boxes on wet Wednesdays in October or sub zero nights in Hartlepool. Yet he knew, if he was honest with himself that he'd been going through the motions for a long time. Sometimes not even that. Often, just cobbling together enough words to justify his right to the company laptop and his place in his work cubicle that had become a home from home. That is when he was not covering a game that justified an overnight stay in a Travelodge or some Northern B&B furnished in the council house 'chic' that reminded him of growing up, of the times when he still believed that he could have been someone. Could have been a player. A proper player. Not the Wednesday League no-hoper that he had turned out to be.

"Look Brian, you've got two weeks to sort yourself out. I can't carry any passengers anymore. I want you to drop everything and find Christie. Find out what's going on there. I want this story. You're going to get it for me, but you can't mess about. Everybody will be on Christie's trail now."

"I'd love to, but I've got the Villa game to cover tomorrow, so . . ."

"Forget the Villa game. Forget everything. Find Christie, get the story and we'll see about keeping you on. Get it."

"Ummm . . . Got it."

CHAPTER FOUR
BOW BELLS

"Get a life you loser."

Jonathan looked out from the west bound District Line train as two twenty-somethings, all stilettos and push up bras, teetered on their heels. Buoyed by the closing of the train doors they continued their abuse.

"Yeah. Get a proper job" said one as the other cupped her right hand, placed it on the top of her head and began an up and down stroking motion, which he knew only too well to be the universal symbol for 'Knobhead'.

"I have got a proper job" he muttered and looked to the handful of other passengers for reassurance. Opposite, the guy in the tight fitting shiny suit ran three fingers through his tousled hair, made fleeting eye contact, raised half an eyebrow in support, then buried himself in the pages of his copy of *The New Yorker*.

It was as if most of the other passengers were getting ready to go into an exam about mobile phones or cheap calls to Australia and New Zealand as they stared unflinchingly at the banner adverts in a last minute frenzy of revision.

A large Nigerian lady balanced a correspondingly large blue and white striped plastic holdall on her lap, bit her bottom lip and gave him sideways glances as she puffed and grimaced, rummaging around in the bag. Ceasing her rummaging for a moment, she poked her face through the crumpled arch made by the bag handles, looking like an advert for the Lagos branch of McDonalds.

"Hold on my son. I got something for you in here. You take no notice o' dem. You're doin' a good job. Where would we be without you guys?"

He tried to think of a suitable response but she halted his train of thought.

"I tell you where we would be. Stuck at home watching *Strictly Come Dancing* that's where. How would I get out o' that shitty tower block to do The Lord's work if there were no trains eh?"

Catching a glimpse of his brown calf length work boots, he followed a line upwards along his tucked in half mast trousers, up to his hi-viz jacket then rested his gaze on the faded Transport for London logo on his left breast. The shaven headed one with the earpiece had thought he'd done the deal of the century when he swapped Jonathan's goalkeeping kit for some old tat that was lying around in the back office. He was so happy he even threw in a one-day Travelcard for good measure.

"Oh I get it" said Jonathan "You think I'm . . ."

THE ART OF BEING ONE

"I don't think, I know my son. You is an angel of God. I spotted it as soon as you got on. You got that look. Now let me just find that pamphlet, it's in here somewhere."

She dived even deeper dipping her whole face into the top of the bag as if bobbing for apples.

"He's no angel." A wild-eyed ponytailed drunk jerked out of a half sleep looking as washed out as his faded claret and blue West Ham shirt which bore the name of a sponsor long since defunct.

"He's Jesus he is ain't ya?"

He ran a shaking hand across the base of his nose and wiped away a drip.

"Yeees" he slurred straining his neck in Jonathan's direction "Yers alright Jesus? He's JC he is missus."

Holding his gaze for a moment, Jonathan slid his hand into his jacket pocket. He rubbed his fingers along his one-day Travelcard, and to avoid the drunk's attentions began to read it as if absorbed in a pageturner.

The battle with the bag continued. "I know I put it in here. I had it on the kitchen table next to my big book of Sudoku"

"He's come to save us ain't ya? Ain't ya JC?" the drunk's head lolled backwards as if he had lost interest in his monologue until the train jerked his head forward again.

"He's going to make everything alright. Everything's... gonna...be...all right" he said clenching his fist and making a half-hearted attempt at a gesture of solidarity.

A small tear welled up in the corner of Jonathan's eye, unprompted, unexpected, unexplained. It teetered as if holding onto a ledge, held in place by a supportive eyelid, only to trickle quickly along his cheek, before pausing and dropping onto the 'T' of his Travelcard.

He stared at this small bubble of liquid for a moment and watched it melt into the thin cream coloured card, then rubbed it away with his index finger. He rubbed a second time, and watched the ink smear so as to convert the 'T' into the shape of a cross.

The train slowed as it drew into Bow Station. There was shriek and a grunt and a 'coming together' as the drunk and the Nigerian leaned in towards their prey. The stripy bag hit the floor. An Afro comb; the dog eared big book of Sudoku; a silver tin foil package that looked like it contained a large hand grenade; a book of cerise coloured raffle tickets; several crumpled Lidl bags; miscellaneous small packets of sugar; a Rubiks cube neatly showing the final solution; a couple of pens that looked like they had once belonged on a National Lottery point of sale unit; half a dozen sticks with cotton wool ends, some tinged with the honey brown of earwax; and a small pamphlet with a crude line drawing of Jesus pinned to a cross.

A size 13 boot left a tyre tread mark on the Jesus pamphlet as Jonathan upped and headed for the doors.

The woman with the stripy bag headlocked the drunk and squeezed him down to his knees.

"You don't touch my stuff. Now put it all back in my bag . . . no you don't touch my stuff"

Jonathan glanced back at the commotion and the tyre trodden Jesus.

The drunk grimaced.

"Help me Jesus, she's choking meee."

She lightened her grip. The drunk in a kneeling position began what sounded like a football chant, clapping in between his words.

"JEEEZUS" clap, clap, clap "JEEEZUS" clap, cl. .a . . . p, cla . . .

The clapping faded as Jonathan skipped onto the platform and took the stairs three at a time.

The guy in the shiny suit glanced up, ran a few fingers through his tousled hair then lost himself in *The New Yorker*.

CHAPTER FIVE
MEET MR MOONBOOTS

Brian Dugdale collected the small rucksack that he kept under his desk, containing the single change of clothes that he had cobbled together whilst his soon to be ex-wife had reeled off a long list of his faults and failings during his last visit home.

He flipped the rucksack onto his back, turned and strode from the cubicle before stooping and walking back in again. He thought for a moment. Find Christie. This was uncharted territory. This wasn't going through the motions at Stoke City or Blackburn. This was going to need some serious thought.

There was only one person that Dugdale turned to when serious thought was needed, or indeed, when any form of thought, serious or otherwise, was needed. Moonboots.

To the casual observer, Moonboots appeared to have taken up residence in The Black Lion in Plaistow High Street, rarely moving more than one or two elbow lengths from his regular position at the arc of the bar. From here he could scan the morning papers, laid out for him by the bar staff, because that's what they had always done. A glance to the right offered him a view of Sky Sports, whilst, if he craned his neck slightly to the left, he could catch a glimpse of the 24 hour rolling news on a screen in an adjoining room.

He cut an eccentric figure. Probably in his late fifties, he had lost the hair on top of his head, but kept the sides long and stringy, still jet-black, down on to the shoulder of his black three quarter length leather overcoat. His outfit never changed. A black crew neck jumper, straining a bit around the paunch, tucked into faded black jeans, which in turn tucked into the calf length high lace boots. The 'moonboots' that had ensured him a place as a legend amongst a couple of handfuls of Black Lion regulars.

The thing about Moonboots that endeared and irritated in equal measure was his ability to speak at length on any topic. By 1pm he had been through all of the Black Lion's newspapers, mostly red tops, but occasionally he would pick up a Guardian or an Independent left by a passing salesman or a more erudite member of the university's Real Ale Society. In the afternoon he would follow the horse racing, rarely having a bet, but knowing enough about form to be able to advise the other drinkers on what they should have done. His perfect positioning between two 42-inch plasmas ensured that he was up to date with the latest in sport and current affairs, so that by the time the early evening drinkers arrived he was ready to go on any subject that might arise.

It was well known amongst the regular drinkers that it was unwise to let Moonboots get onto anything vaguely to do with planets, aliens, other worldly creatures, the occult or conspiracy theories. Not unless you had a couple of hours to idle away. Occasionally some wandering, lone drinker would fall into his trap and be too polite or befuddled to stop him. With glazed eyes, they'd nod in polite agreement until finishing the last quarter of their pint in one go, shaking Moonboots hand and making a dash for the door.

"Pint of Viking Old Peculiar for me, and give Moonboots what he wants" Dugdale wheezed as he bent to balance his backpack on the brass foot rail hugging the lower part of the bar.

Moonboots feigned an upper class accent "Thank you my man. Landlord, I'll have a flagon of your best Dunham Market Gold in a pothandle."

"Listen Moonboots, get your pint and come and sit down."

"Sit down?" Moonboots looked around at the empty seats, save for a couple enjoying a flirtatious after work drink. He looked back at his usual place by the bar. "Why would I want to sit down? I never sit down."

"Look, I bought you a pint didn't I? Come and sit down, I need the benefit of your opinion."

Moonboots raised an eyebrow. He liked the sound of this. Opinions were his meat and drink. He surveyed the seating area once more, nodded and began to stride towards a banquette, raising up the skirt of his three quarter length leather overcoat and then sitting with what appeared to be a great leather parcel on his lap.

Dugdale squeezed in opposite him. "Cheers." Both men took a large gulp from their glasses and then stared down momentarily into the froth, savouring the flavours and aromas like a couple of old wine buffs.

Moonboots broke the silence "Villa" he said.

"Eh?" Dugdale looked up quizzically.

"Villa. You wanted my opinion. You're covering the Villa match tomorrow. Villa will win 3-1 and it'll be 1-1 at half time."

"No it's not that . . . and I'm not covering the Villa match, not anymore. It's about the keeper that did a runner. Christie."

Moonboots stroked the pathetic wisps of hair around the tip of his chin that were the closest thing he could get to a goatee. "Ah, the mysterious Mr Christie eh?"

"Yes. What would possess someone to just walk off during a match? Why would he do that? Where did he go? Where is he now?" Dugdale took another sip of his Viking Old Peculiar and two vertical lines appeared above the bridge of his nose as he pondered these questions.

"Brian, my dear friend it's obvious. It's a good thing you're not in the investigative branch of journalism. You'd better stick to writing those arcane match reports. I'll bet you've already written the Villa one for tomorrow. I know your trick. You just cut and paste your standard phrases and change the names" Moonboots winked and gave Dugdale a knowing tilt of the head.

Dugdale spluttered on a mouthful of beer "Obvious. What do you mean obvious?"

THE ART OF BEING ONE

Moonboots picked up his near empty glass and stood up "Let's repair to the bar Brian. Your round."

With the glasses were recharged, Moonboots assumed his familiar leaning pose in his established territory.

"Go on" Dugdale said impatiently.

"Think about it Brian. The lad's earning a small fortune. Bored. Nothing to spend his money on. A lot of time to kill. He's playing in the East End. What's the East End famous for?"

"Cockneys?"

"Mmmm. Try again."

"Curries?"

"Come on Brian. What is the East End *notorious* for?"

"Come on Moonboots just spit it out."

Moonboots wasn't in the habit of spitting things out if he felt he could make a story last for another pint or two.

"The Krays, The Richardsons, Mad Frankie Fraser . . . am I making any sense . . . ?"

"No you're not making any sense. So the East End is notorious for being the home of gangsters, but what's that got to do with Christie?"

"The song. The 'bubble' song."

"So what? They've been singing 'I'm forever blowing bubbles' at West Ham for as long as anyone can remember."

"But you were there Brian. I was watching it in here as usual. You must have noticed. They changed the song. They replaced the name of the visiting team with the name of the visiting goalkeeper. They never do that. Never."

Moonboots placed his hands flat on the bar, leaned back slightly, pointed his chin upwards and gently closed his eyelids.

He hammed up a cockney accent and began to sing in a surprisingly sweet high-pitched voice.

> "I'm forever blowing bubbles,
> Pretty bubbles in the air,
> They fly so high,
> Nearly reach the sky . . .

At this point he raised his right hand from the bar and pinched together the tips of his index finger and thumb and made small circular movements as if he were guiding an invisible piece of chalk across an imaginary blackboard.

> "Like *Jonathan Christie* they fade and die."

Still with eyes closed, he made a grand gesture of inserting the full stop with his fingers. For a moment, he remained still, before snapping his eyes open as if emerging from some deep hypnotic slumber.

Dugdale stood open mouthed. As much irritated by Moonboots cryptic responses as taken aback that such a sweet sound come out of the mouth of the weird one.

"Very nice Moonboots, but Christie's had a long career. He's heard every insult that there is. Why would he take umbrage at his name being in the 'bubbles' song?"

"My theory is that he was being given a message" said Moonboots downing the rest of his pint in one, holding his glass in the air and looking towards Dugdale expectantly.

"Hmmmph. This is the last one Moonboots. Just get to the point"

"So. The lad's bored. He's got too much time on his hands, too much money. He starts having a flutter. Harmless fun at first, then it gets out of hand. Soon he's in hock to a 'face', as I believe they are called in the movies. Serious debt with serious gangsters. They decide to give him a message . . . he's gonna die. He hears the song, thinks someone in the crowd is about to take a pot shot at him, then he does one. That's it."

Moonboots took a large swig of Viking Old Peculiar, banged his glass on the bar and belched.

CHAPTER SIX
YOU CAN CALL ME DAZ

Jonathan leapt the barrier at Bow Station. His one-day Travelcard didn't seem to open the turnstile when he swiped it over the Oyster Card reader the way he had seen other people do it, and he panicked when he saw the guard coming in his direction. A step back, a giant leap and a roll on the concrete bounced him up into the goalkeeper's ready position.

He stood alert for a few moments as if expecting an in-coming free kick, then as the ticket collectors gathered their thoughts, he sprinted into the East London night.

It had been years since he'd been in a church. Not since the Sunday Morning service at the kid's home, but Bow church was an open door to run into. An exile from the chasing pack of ticket collectors, drunks and large Nigerian ladies that he imagined were frantically following in his wake. He peered out into the street through a gap in the door before gently and quietly bringing it to a close.

"We tend to leave the door open here." Reverend Darren, a short, grey suited man with a thin pink tie stood in the vestry doorway bearing the smile of an insincere salesman.

"Yeah, but there's a few dodgy people out there mate" said Jonathan.

"Dodgies; weirdos; outsiders; insiders; odd people; pod people; loners; moaners; they're all welcome here. That door never closes." He tilted his head still holding his smile.

Jonathan pulled the door slightly ajar and peeped out into the street.

"Expecting somebody?" the Reverend asked.

"I'm not sure" said Jonathan "I just wanted a place to sit; to think. To be honest mate, I'm not sure where I'm going really."

"If you don't know where you're going any road will do." The Reverend pursed his lips and winked.

"You've got to hand it to Jesus. He had an answer for everything didn't he?" shrugged Jonathan.

"That wasn't Jesus. It was Lewis Carroll. Alice in Wonderland. Talking of tea parties, fancy a cuppa?"

The vestry armchair hugged Jonathan's tall frame like a long lost friend. He held the chipped London Olympics mug to his lips and slurped.

"Hey, hold on. This isn't like a confessional is it?"

Reverend Darren pushed his buttocks against the battered wooden desk and slid up into a seated position. His short legs wavered backwards and forwards in the gap between the desk drawers before slowing to a halt.

"That's the other team over the road. They like that sort of thing. But if there's something you want to say . . ."

"Like what? Like I don't know where I'm going or what I'm doing? Like I'm probably unemployable now? Like my brain feels like it's frazzled? That sort of thing?"

"You don't have to say anything" Darren said.

"Like I'm angry. Like I feel like a total loser?"

Jonathan banged his cup on the coffee table on the 'r' of 'loser'. The Reverend held an awkward silence as Jonathan gazed at his work boots.

"I'm sorry mate. It's not your fault. I just feel so . . . you know?."

"You can call me Daz. May I call you . . . ?"

There was a sullen nod. "JC. Yeah it's JC. That's what they call me at work. Well they used to."

"You see JC I don't buy this 'loser' thing. I always say 'You were born to win. But to be a winner, you have to plan to win, prepare to win and believe you can win'." He held up a finger at each point and sat looking triumphant with three fingers in the air.

"Yeah well, Jesus should have thought of that when he took on Pontius Pilate. Didn't win that one did he?"

"That wasn't one of Jesus' sayings. That was Zig Ziglar. The greatest salesman that ever lived. We're all salesmen now you know."

Reverend Darren saw himself as a salesman. A purveyor of hope and happiness; a service provider for the bereaved and lonely; a pedlar of ceremonial events of the marriage kind, mostly for non-believers; and a business incubator for the soul. He even had his own Key Performance Indicators, a throwback to his previous life in The City. A life he walked away from the day he finally realised that he had spent a decade selling more than just financial products and derivatives. He was on the verge of selling his own soul.

He still liked to be 'target driven' though, and a series of line graphs, bar charts and pie diagrams were blu-tacked to the wall behind him, showing his progress – attendances; donations per head; income generation; christenings; weddings; funerals; food programme beneficiaries; and so on. On a whiteboard he had written in thick red marker pen the words 'Outcomes not Outputs'. It was difficult for him to shake off the business culture that he had grown up in, so he decided just to embrace it. He'd had a small column in the *Money* section of *The Independent* for a couple of years, where his main claim to fame was his calculation of how the man in the street could become a millionaire just by taking up their annual ISA allowance and using the power of compound interest. He called it his 'reap what you sow' moment.

"I'm sorry I flipped out then" Jonathan said "In church like. I shouldn't have done that. I just find myself wanting revenge all the time. That's wrong isn't it?"

THE ART OF BEING ONE

"It's normal JC, completely normal. I don't know what you want revenge for. I don't need to know. You'd expect me to say 'Turn the other cheek' I suppose. That's what Jesus would have said. You see, Jesus was a good guy, but he just didn't grasp the power of compound interest. That's why the world's in the state it's in."

Darren slid off the desk and rubbed the whiteboard clean. He sketched out a matrix and drew a column 1-20 then pulled a pound coin from his pocket held it up and slammed it on the desktop.

"Now imagine you invested this one pound, for say twenty years at an interest rate of say 5%. How much would you have at the end of the twenty years?"

"I don't know. Not much. Maybe two or three quid? What's this got to do with Jesus?"

The marker pen squeaked as Darren drew an elaborate pound sign followed by 2.52. He planted a dramatic full stop at the end.

"I'll come to that later. But that's not a bad answer. It's actually £2.52."

"So what?" Jonathan lifted the Velcro pocket in his hi-viz jacket and checked that his Travelcard was still there.

"So what?" Darren walked back in front of his desk and spread his arms as if trying to put off a penalty taker. "So what? That's 152% growth that is. It's amazing."

"No. It's £2.52 mate" said Jonathan glancing over to the door and wondering how best he could work his way towards it.

"If you change the pound to a hundred pounds that's £252. If you invested a million that's two million five hundred and twenty thousand. You've made £1.5 million just by reinvesting."

"I'm gonna have to go soon mate" Jonathan stood and towered over Darren. He placed a comforting arm on his shoulder "But that's really good Daz. Better than £2.52 anyway."

The Reverend seemed determined not to lose his audience. "No it's exactly the same. The principle is the same whatever the amount. Sit down a minute. I'll do another brew. This is important. We'll have a biscuit."

Jonathan did as he was asked and pulled a tin box of Teatime Assorted from a high cupboard above the kettle and assembled a batch of biscuits on a chipped white plate.

"I'm sorry mate. I just don't get it. I'll have a biscuit then I'm off" Jonathan said, reluctantly resuming his position in the armchair.

Darren came closer and squatted on the coffee table in front of Jonathan, leaning in as though about to impart a secret.

"So this is where Jesus and I disagree. He would say if you've been wronged 'Turn the other cheek'. In other words be wronged again. Ha! That's like letting somebody make a withdrawal from your bank of goodwill and then inviting them to make another withdrawal. I say if you are wronged you should make a deposit not a withdrawal. Invest some goodwill. Goodwill is like leaving your interest in the bank. It creates more goodwill. Jesus was in favour of depleting his assets . . . the bible makes that quite clear . . . I'm in favour of investing and reinvesting . . . that's why he was . . ."

Darren looked over his shoulder towards the door, leaned closer and lowered his voice.

THE ART OF BEING ONE

." . . That's why he was . . ." he coughed gently and rubbed his palms against his thighs ." . . a loser."

Darren stood up and paced around the office. His face a mixture of elation and embarrassment as if he had relieved himself of a great burden and then thought better about it.

"Thanks for the tea mate" said Jonathan with one hand on the doorknob. "I wish I knew what you were on about, I really do, but I've got my own issues at the moment. I don't even know where I'm gonna kip tonight."

Handing his business card to Jonathan, the Reverend directed him to a Christian hostel by the side of St Paul's Cathedral, just a few stops on the Central Line.

"Give them my card. Tell them Daz sent you. You'll be alright for a night or two there." Just for good measure he pulled a ten-pound note from his wallet and wrapped it around the card. "Oh and remember that famous saying? 'Everything will be all right when it's over. If it's not all right it's not over'. Look after yourself JC."

He nodded "Was that the Ziggy fella that said that or was that Jesus?"

Darren clasped his hands together as if in prayer.

"John Lennon. More famous than Jesus Christ."

The door closed and he turned to his wall to fill in another coloured block on a chart headed 'Hostel referrals'.

As Jonathan trecked back in the direction of Bow Station, a crazed out of breath, ponytailed man in faded claret and blue burst into the Reverend's office.

"I've seen him Daz. I've seen him. Jesus is alive. He works on the tube."

CHAPTER SEVEN
LITTLE ITALY

Roberto Capriolo strode onto the training pitch wearing his trademark tracksuit and padded overcoat, his hands dug deep into his pockets, head bowed determinedly forward, until he reached the centre circle. He signaled to the coaches to bring the players together and made them sit on the very edge of the centre circle going to great lengths to make sure that everybody sat outside the white line, so that not even a bootlace impinged his private space.

He walked around the full circle, making sure that his quiet anger was transmitted through the bodies of all the players, who began to cease their chatter as he caught their eye with his unmistakable glare. Returning to the centre of the circle, he held out his palms and paddled them up and down to make a calming gesture, until there was absolute silence.

For a moment he looked up at the sky, as though seeking

some inspiration, then began a walk which zigzagged and turned across his circular domain so that he was able to meet the eyes of every player at some point.

"You see these men?" he pointed to his group of coaches "Marco, Giovanni, Paolo, Little Roberto, Fredo. These men, and don't forget the ones inside who look after you. Ivan, the fitness guy, the head physio and so on and so on" He stood motionless for a moment and paused.

"All Italian" he clenched his fist "All with me at every club I manage" he clenched his other fist and brought them together in front of him. "You know why? It's because we are like family. We win together, we lose together. We laugh together, we cry together. We live together . . . we die together. That is how we are."

He pointed to a squat Uruguayan.

"Fanni stand up and come out here."

The little South American raised his knees up and leant backwards, pushing up with his arms from his seated position, so that he did a little flip that ejected him forward into the centre circle like an acrobat leaping into a circus ring.

Capriolo looked Fanni in the eyes, and pulled a plain brown wooden pencil from his pocket "Fanni, here is a pencil. I want to see if you can break it."

Fanni, sensing that this was some kind of trick, and that he was about to be the fall guy, looked at the pencil in disbelief for a moment and then followed the instructions. Holding the two ends of the pencil, he snapped it in two pieces and then shrugged his shoulders. There were cheers from the rest of the players and a shout from one of them "Told you Fanni had no lead in his pencil" which brought even more cheers.

"STOP. YOU STOP" barked Capriolo returning to his angry state. Silence prevailed once again and he turned slowly looking through the faces for Fanni's fellow Uruguayan "Mushi, now you come up here." Mushi was a bit taller than Fanni and didn't attempt to compete with his acrobatic leap, instead he walked up slowly, chewing an imaginary piece of gum.

Capriolo reached in to his pocket a second time "Now, Mushi. Here are eleven pencils. I want you to try to break them."

Mushi took all eleven pencils in both hands trying to look nonchalant, as he attempted to break the pack, which brought a few sniggers from the rest of the squad. Determined not to lose face, he began to take the challenge more seriously, bending trying to use his thigh as a fulcrum, grimacing and hoping that brute force would win the day. He bent one way then another, finally taking a deep breath in one last attempt to find a weakness in the pack.

Capriolo stood with his arms folded, occasionally checking the progress of Mushi, but mostly examining the expressions on the faces of the players, crushing a snigger or a quip with an icy glare.

Mushi stopped after his final gallant attempt to deploy brute force. Capriolo was pleased that Mushi had tried so hard to break the pencils and failed. Mushi though, would not be beaten. He gave Capriolo a petulant stare, then placed the pencils between his knees and pushed his legs together so that the insides of his kneecaps held them in a vice-like grip. One by one, he pulled a pencil from the pack and snapped it, before throwing it on the ground. The first one slowly and deliberately staring at Capriolo as if to say "Whose the smartarse now?" Then the pace quickened until Mushi was snapping and throwing pencils onto the floor with such force and anger it was like watching a child's uncontrollable tantrum.

By the time the eleventh pencil had hit the floor, Mushi's face had turned bright red and he was breathing heavily. He stood straight, pushed his shoulders back and took a step forward towards Capriolo as if daring him to issue another challenge.

Capriolo remained with his arms folded. Unmoved, unperturbed he stared at Mushi for a while and then said "Thank you Mushi. Go back to your place now."

There was a look of disappointment from Mushi. Somehow he felt he should have been applauded for finding a solution.

"Now you listen. Is very important. You see how easy it is to break one pencil the way that Fanni did. How difficult it is to break eleven pencils. Mushi showed us that if you divide the pencils you can break them all, but together is impossible to break."

He beckoned all of the players and invited them to cross the previously un-crossable white line and come inside the centre circle. The coaches were positioned so that they stood up on the edge of the circle forming a kind of fortress wall, with the players seated inside.

"This is our family. Inside these walls, inside this fortress we are one family. Alone we can be broken. Together nothing can break us."

He strolled over to where the standing group were assembled and walked past three or four of them staring deeply into their eyes like a Sergeant Major looking for any indication of weakness or betrayal, before turning back to face the group.

"There is one opportunity I offer now to any one of you. If you don't want to be in the family is okay. You leave this circle now. We make you a transfer. We find you a loan, give you a sick note . . . whatever. If you stay in this circle you are family. We will not be broken. We live together . . . we die together. So, I turn my back. Anyone is not part of the family leave now . . . Little Roberto will sort everything out for you."

This was a gamble. He couldn't afford to lose Fanni or Mushi in particular at this crucial stage of the season, yet he knew if anyone left the circle he would have to be seen to follow through his actions. He put his arms behind his back and looked up to the sky, closing his eyes for thirty seconds, hoping that this was not a gamble too far. Nobody moved.

"Good. We are together in this. They are trying to break us. One person, Jonathan has left the family. After this we talk of him no more. They will not break us if we stay together. You will hear some things over the next days . . . allegations . . . whatever. They are designed to try to break us . . . the team, the project . . . the family. Jonathan is not part of the family. Fanni and Mushi are. Whatever you hear, we support the family."

A smile spread across his face.

"OK now we turn to our old ally 'repetition' we do some work on shape" This brought some good natured groans from a couple of the younger players, broadening his smile "And you boys will stay behind with me today. I'll find some more repetition for you to do."

As the player's dispersed, Mushi hovered around the centre circle and Capriolo placed an arm around his shoulders.

"Mushi my friend, you want me to find some more pencils for you to break?"

"No boss. What is this thing I hear you say before. Old aleea? Old alloy? What does it mean?"

"Ah you mean 'ally'. Let me see . . . it is a kind of . . . Amici. A friend who can be relied upon"

"Ah I see boss. So you are my ally right?"

"Mushi my friend, when you are fighting for my cause I am your biggest ally. When you are not fighting for my cause I am your worst enemy."

CHAPTER EIGHT
ALL CHANGE FOR EPPING

They call it the 'Northerner's error'.

It's easily done, especially if the tube is not your normal stomping ground.

A small rumble began under Jonathan's feet.

He'd slipped back into Bow Station, unwrapped his Travelcard from the ten-pound note that Reverend Darren had slipped into his hand, and this time managed to put it into the right slot. He felt bad about taking the ten quid – a man with a thirteen million pound investment portfolio, but he took it anyway. Just in case.

The rumble grew louder as a train approached and then

pulled into the platform. Two middle aged couples ran down the stairs making encouraging gestures and noises to each other, the men pulling the women along like climbers descending a perilous mountain slope, determined to make the train.

Registering their urgency he followed suit jumping onto the train just as the doors closed.

He slouched on a seat and began to read the banner adverts offering loans at unfeasibly high rates of interest and tried to calculate what would happen to Reverend Darren's one pound after 20 years at 1037% APR. Not that he knew what APR meant. He struggled with the size of the numbers, before concluding that perhaps it didn't matter as long as you paid it back before April.

An hour later he learned that he had made the 'Northener's error'. Since time immemorial, the London tube system has been littered with Northerners who took the eastbound when they wanted the westbound or the southbound when they were headed north. The sound of an oncoming train just as they were approaching the platform seeming to disengage their brains until they reached some outlying clone town or a leafy suburb miles from where they were meant to be.

A weary looking guard popped his head through the door and into the compartment.

"Can't sleep here mate. All change for Epping."

Startled, Jonathan opened his eyes and tried to focus.

"Eh? Nah . . . I'm going to St Pauls mate. Is this St Pauls?"

"You ain't going nowhere mate. This is Epping. End of the line. No more trains till tomorrow."

"Epping? What's at Epping?"
"Forest mate. Miles and miles of frigging forest."

The next time Jonathan awoke he was lying in a small ditch in the forest floor. Cold and covered in pieces of cardboard that he'd found in a skip. There was something bearing down on the centre of his forehead. More than the onset of a headache, it felt like a miniature icepack. As he gently opened and lifted his eyes to try to see the shape of the thing, he felt a tiny vibration.

His right hand whipped across his forehead and he caught the tiny back legs of a frog. Gently cupping the creature he held it in captivity for a moment and stared closely at its tiny face, much smaller than he had imagined a frog to be. It struggled for a moment and then took on a stoic calm, ready to make a giant leap but only when the moment was right.

"You must be a goalkeeper my friend. Waiting for your moment eh? The moment when you're supposed to jump."

They stared into each other's eyes for some time as if they were somehow connected in the chain of evolution. Goalkeeper and frog.

"You're just like me aren't you mate? You just want to be free. Well my jumping days are over pal. I ain't jumping for anyone anymore. But you can."

He eased his grip and the frog sensing the opportunity

made its predicted leap for freedom, using Jonathan's forehead as a springboard.

He tilted his head backwards to try to follow the creature's trajectory with his eyes, but it was gone in an instant. There was a rustling in the foliage and then what sounded like the plucking of a tiny harp. "Was that a musical frog?" he thought "Magical maybe? Here to give me a message or something."

He stiffened as the plucking turned into a long drawl and then a vibrant reel of sound as if a violin were crying out, a brokenhearted cry. He lay still and taut, eyes flitting from side to side, wondering what to do, imagining a small orchestra of frogs performing on the edge of the ditch.

Quietly, so as not to disturb the performance, he slid his cardboard covers to one side, eased himself to his knees and peered through a bank of ferns into a clearing, half expecting to see an ensemble of tuxedoed frogs. He could make out some pinks and greys and a bit of bright yellow and the frantic movement of what appeared to be an elbow, human not frog. The musical reel gathered pace, now, as if the instrument were calling out for help and drawing him towards its cry.

Moving upwards into the clearing he could make out the shape of a tall, slender red headed female, her pink camouflage trousers and yellow hi-visability waterproof jacket standing out against the greens and browns of the forest. She sat, eyes closed, on an old tree stump, leaning to and fro, lost in the haunting sound until she drew three long cries with her bow and picked out the same harp like sound with which she had started.

The forest fell silent. She took three long breaths before slowly opening her eyes to confront Jonathan's imposing frame. She flinched. Her English was good, but the slight elongation of the 's' sounds and the undulation of her voice clearly betrayed an accent.

"Jesus. You scared the shit out of me."

Jonathan took three steps back and raised his hands as if in surrender.

"I'm sorry love. I was just lying in that ditch and heard the music. There was a frog and then the music. I thought it was the frog . . . I mean . . . I don't know what I mean. I just never heard a violin make a noise like that before."

She pouted. "This is not a violin. This is a fiddle. The most special fiddle in the world. It's a Hardanger fiddle, and anyway what are you doing lying in a ditch? What do you mean you thought it was a frog? How many frogs do you know that play the Hardanger fiddle?"

He puffed out his cheeks and thought for a moment.

"Well none. In fact I don't know anyone that plays any kind of music. Well until now." He stretched out his hand and stepped forward "I'm. ."

"Stay there" she said stretching out her bow in sword-like fashion "I can kill a man with this bow. Don't come any closer."

He turned on his heel and moved back to his previous position drawing his hands together in a prayer-like pose.

"Whoa. Look I'm sure you can. Kill a man with that I mean."

"I can" she said proffering her bow at full stretch.

"Look can we just start again? I got a bit lost. I heard your music. It was nice, I really liked it. I just wanted to see where it was coming from that's all. I was just going to introduce myself when I . . ."

"When you lunged at me?" she said standing up without lowering her outstretched bow.

He held out his hand again. "No. That was no lunge. I was just offering to introduce myself honest."

She eyed him up and down then placed her fiddle on the tree stump. "Well I suppose we share the same taste in Hi-viz jackets. You may take a step closer . . . but I won't hesitate to kill you."

Still with his hand outstretched he moved forward a pace or two to be greeted by a fiddle bow pressed hard against his chest. Without moving the bow she stretched out her hand.

"I'm Marrielle" she said "And you are?"

Jonathan stared at her delicate hand for a moment as if he had never shaken hands with anyone before. Then without thinking locked her hand in a grip that made her wince. "JC. They call me JC."

"Ouch JC. Be careful. My hands are my living."

"Me too" he said, opening out his large palms and looking at them as if to make sure they were still there.

"Jesus. What are you? A lumberjack?"

CHAPTER NINE
BACK TO MY ROOTS

Moonboots looked more than vaguely ridiculous as he strode along Green Street and past the street market wearing a black goalkeeper's kit and his trademark calf length boots.

It had taken Dugdale more than the few pints of real ale that it usually took to get Moonboots to move from his base camp in The Black Lion. The promise of an Indian meal with all the trimmings was the thing that finally shifted him. They'd hatched a plan that seemed slightly hair-brained even in their drunken state the night before. Now, watching a balding middle-aged man trying to look like an athletic goalkeeper in an East London street market, brought home to Dugdale just how far his fortunes had sunk.

It was Moonboots that planted the idea. His theory was that Dugdale had nothing to lose. The way he'd described his situation, it seemed almost certain he was going to get sacked anyway. Why let the boss take all the glory if Dugdale managed to get to Christie first? This story could be massive, big enough to sort out his retirement and pay off his wife, maybe even to buy a small place in the sun. All Moonboots wanted was twenty-five percent of whatever the story raised.

A disappearing goalkeeper, gangsters and who knows what else they might uncover? That was the way Moonboots sold the idea. In the hands of the right PR man, they reasoned that this story could be worth £250,000 at least. The drunken haze and the upbeat Bhangra music in the Bombay Palace were filling Dugdale with optimism. This could be his one last chance at glory. A chance to show everyone, his editor, his wife, his sarcastic work colleagues, that he had always had talent. A chance to rub their noses in it. One last chance for the big payday he deserved.

By the time the poppadoms and another bottle of Cobra had slid down they'd concluded that a bidding war would see the value of the story rise to half a million. It was the waiter's good fortune when he brought the bill the figure had risen to cool million, and buoyed by his unexpected good fortune Dugdale left an unusually large tip.

It probably wasn't a good idea to finish the night with a couple of whiskies at Moonboots bedsit. It most certainly wasn't a good idea for Dugdale to email his resignation to his boss at 3am. Full of typos and badly punctuated, his parting shot was to the point, and after he had deleted the abuse that he had really wanted to send, ended up quite succinct and matter of fact.

Reality hit home when Dugdale opened his eyes to a nicotine stained Artex ceiling and seven missed calls on his phone. He prompted the voicemail. It was Merlin Shoesmith. "Brian, I've tried calling you seven times now. I haven't got the time to keep chasing you like this. If I don't hear from you in the next half hour, I'm going to pass your email onto Human Resources. Get in touch quick."

Human Resources had already emailed back, advising Dugdale that he was contractually obliged to serve one month's notice, but his line manager had requested that he serve his notice period on 'gardening leave'. His personal effects would be forwarded to him and he should arrange to come in and for a debriefing session with representatives of the Human Resources Department at his convenience.

"The bastards" he said to no one on particular. "Look at that 'Mr Dugdale'. Not 'Brian', like it was when that snotty bitch wanted me to get two tickets for her husband to go and see shitty Brentford."

When Dugdale got through to Merlin Shoesmith to try to explain, he could feel his now former boss grinning down the phone, as he feigned sympathy "I'm sorry it had to end this way Brian, you know that, but I did everything in my power to stop it. You left me with no choice. As a professional manager, which is what I am essentially, I had a duty to take the advice of HR, you know that. I want to wish you luck in whatever it is you are going to do. What are you going to do?"

"Things" Dugdale said, trying to absorb the reality of the situation and without sounding even more like the loser that

Shoesmith thought he was. "I've got plans. I can't go into detail. I'll be doing things of a literary nature. Setting my sights a bit higher than, you know Merlin, a bit higher than the sort of stuff you do." He felt that he'd got in a nice little jab there.

"Ha" Shoesmith exclaimed "I'll keep my eyes on the short-list for The Nobel Prize for Literature Brian."

That was it. The end of a career, if you could call it that. There was a sense of relief for Dugdale, mingled with a tinge of fear. Two more paydays and he would be on his own. Too old to get another job in the business, too tired to charge around for freelance money.

There was a scratching noise at the front door followed by a lot of fumbling before Moonboots fell in carrying a pint of milk and a small pensioner's style sliced loaf.

"You know what Moonboots?" Dugdale said steeling himself against the unknown "I know we were pissed last night, but someone's going to find Christie. Someone's going to get that story, an exclusive. Someone's going to make an absolute fortune. Why not? Why shouldn't it be me?"

"Us" Moonboots interrupted "Us. It was my idea remember?"

"Yes. That's what I meant. Us. We are all in this together, as they say . . . now about your other idea. The reconstruction."

Moonboots was beginning to regret being a big fan of *Crimewatch*. He had explained to Dugdale that the best results came when they did a reconstruction of the events leading to the crime, or sometimes a disappearance, like this one. Often, as Moonboots had unwisely pointed out, the person doing the reconstruction of events bore little resemblance to the actual person. That's how he ended up wearing a football kit for the first time since he was a twelve year old.

"Just think of the money Moonboots" Dugdale called out as he walked behind him "A million quid. You won't look so stupid then."

There was a great peel of laughter from a vegetable stall, as the vendor nodded towards Moonboots and his customers turned to stare "Ere, you wait all week for a goalkeeper to come along, then two come along at once . . ." he shouted. There was a further round of laughter as the line of customers rocked hysterically.

Moonboots strolled on as Dugdale went and verified that Christie had actually walked this way two days earlier. "Keep going Moonboots, it's working. He went this way down to the tube."

"He could have jumped in a taxi" Moonboots said hoping to draw an end to the proceedings.

"He could, but he was still in his full kit, which suggests that he hadn't been in the dressing rooms. He'd have got changed surely if he had. Anyway, the dressing rooms would have been locked."

"So" Moonboots said, now warming to his role as lead detective "Let's get this straight. He's walked straight off the pitch. No money, no phone, no nothing. Out into the street towards the tube, then he just seems to disappear."

"That seems to be about it. Maybe he jumped the tube. If

he's been down the tube station, someone must remember seeing a grown man in a football kit."

"Hang on" Moonboots interrupted "There were probably about 30,000 people wearing football shirts on Saturday."

"True, but most would have been West Ham shirts, with beer guts like yours. This lad's six feet two", an athlete and in a goalkeeper's kit, the full monty. You won't see many of them around here."

There was a mixture of mirth and suspicion when Dugdale started to make enquiries amongst the ticket collectors and guards at Upton Park Tube station.

"Who's asking?" a bored guard asked leaning against a turnstile "And what's Max Wall doing over there?" he nodded towards Moonboots who stood some distance away trying to look inconspicuous. "If you're from The Sun you can do one."

Dugdale tried hard to placate the guard, "No we're researching a piece for TV, we might do a bit of a reconstruction, that's why he's here, just so we could have a look at camera angles and stuff like that. Listen, there's twenty quid in for you if you can remember anything. You might even get a slot on telly."

"Nah." The guard looked offended "It'd have to be fifty, and even then I can't promise anything. I'd have to speak to Norm you see, he did the thing with the keeper."

"What thing?"

"Like I say, I'd have to speak to Norm about it."

The fifty quid changed hands and the guard returned with a shaven headed colleague whom he introduced as Norm.

Norm looked Dugdale up and down warily. "I hear you're

interested in my friend Mr Christie. What's the story with him?"

"Nobody knows where he is, what's happened, why? We're trying to piece it all together . . . you know, for the TV. Did you see anything? Did he say anything to you?"

"I might have something of interest" Norm said teasingly "But it'll cost you."

Dugdale looked at the other guard and before he could say anything the guard jumped in "I told you, I couldn't promise anything. I said I'd speak to Norm and I did."

Norm took Dugdale's last fifty quid and led him and Moonboots into a pokey little window paneled office. They pulled up an odd assortment of plastic and wooden chairs, whilst Norm bent to unlock the bottom draw of a metal desk.

"Here we go" said Norm "Mr Jonathan Christie's clobber. Everything except those pansy little vests that they wear under their shirts these days, he kept that on. Signed everything else though. Proper gentleman, just looked a bit spaced out."

Jonathan had signed and dated his shirt, shorts, gloves, shin pads and boots. His socks were there too but unsigned and Norm held them as if presenting them to an expert panel on The Antiques Road Show.

"Swapped 'em for a load of old 'tfl' kit that we were going chuck out. I'm going to have this stuff mounted see if I can get a few quid on eBay."

Moonboots, who had sat in a kind of embarrassed silence chipped in. "I wouldn't do that mate. If this story breaks the way we think it will, that stuff could auction for a fortune."

Norm suddenly saw Moonboots in a new light, and offered up pieces of kit for him to inspect more closely.

The signature was pretty consistent on each item of kit, and Moonboots gave Norm advice on how to display each piece and the type of frame that would show them off to their best effect, despite never having had anything framed in his life. They turned to the subject, of what to do with the shinpads. An interesting item, if you like that sort of thing, but hardly beautiful or fascinating enough to adorn your living room wall. Moonboots, tried placing them at different angles to try to get a feel for what might make a pleasing display so that he might advise Norm on the best way forward. Norm watched Moonboots, nodding enthusiastically at each of his suggestions.

"Hmmmm" Moonboots looked carefully at the inside of the left shinpad "Have you seen this? He's written 'Going back to my roots'. Did he say anything about that?"

Norm looked up at the ceiling and thought for a moment "No. He hardly said anything. Didn't strike me as someone who'd be into soul music"

"Soul music?" Dugdale interrupted.

Moonboots and Norm looked at each other, and as though it was a well-rehearsed routine, let out a chorus of "Going back to my roots yeah . . .."

Dugdale tried to get them back on track. "So that was it. He signed his clobber got changed then what, where did he go?"

Norm stood up and moved over to the large underground map that covered the back wall of the office. "Could have gone anywhere with that Travelcard I gave him. You can get from here to anywhere on the system if you know what you're doing."

THE ART OF BEING ONE

Norm began a long routine of all the possible routes and combinations of routes that Jonathan could have taken from Upton Park, before Moonboots gently interrupted "Norm, Norm, can I just stop you there?" Norm was part way through explaining one of the trickiest journeys from Upton Park, the route to Cockfosters involving five changes, unless you took the route via Barking and Blackhorse Road. "Norm. We have to assume that Christie didn't know what he was doing. He's a Northerner for a start."

"Hey hang on . . ." said Dugdale feeling that he had to stand up for Northerners.

"No Brian, what I mean is, he won't be used to the tube system, they don't have them up there do they? And when did you last see a top football player on the underground?"

"Aso-Akota" said Norm knowingly. "You know the French lad, played for Spurs. He used the tube."

"Okay" Moonboots conceded, "One player in the history of The Premier League has been on the tube. I think it would be fair to assume that Christie is a novice as far as the tube is concerned. So what would a novice do?"

Norm rubbed his chin "Hard to tell. If you start changing trains and you don't know what you're doing you could end up anywhere. Safer to stay on one line, in which case he could be anywhere between Upminster and Richmond."

"Well that narrows it down a bit" Dugdale said in frustration.

Moonboots was more upbeat "Hold on Brian. Hold on. At least now we have some kind of a fix on him. He could have been anywhere before. But where's he going?"

"Back to his roots probably" said Norm holding up Jonathan's left shinpad.

CHAPTER TEN
SWEETER THAN HALMUND BJØRGUM

"Do you have to do that?" Jonathan said, nodding at the fiddle bow that Marrielle continued to push hard against his chest.

"You might be an axe murderer for all I know. Lumberjacks are always playing about with axes."

He chuckled. "I'm no lumberjack Marrielle. I'm just a goalkeeper who got a bit lost. Walked off the pitch. Don't know why. Don't know where I'm going."

She lowered her bow and slowly began to walk around

him as if he were a prisoner of war pending interrogation.

"So . . . Mr Goalkeeper. Why are you working on the tube and searching for musical frogs in the forest?"

"I'm not" he said looking down at his 'tfl' uniform as if it had just appeared out of nowhere. "I can explain the gear. I can explain everything. Well everything except the musical frog. Anyway, why are you sitting on a tree stump waking people up with your violin?"

"Fiddle" she said indignantly.

"OK. Fiddle."

"Hardanger fiddle" she said by way of correction.

He looked carefully at the instrument, its gleaming patina contrasting sharply with the rough bark of the tree stump. "Can I hold it? I'll be careful . . . honest"

"You may, but be very gentle lumberjack as she is my most precious possession, and remember I can kill you with a single thrust of my bow" she smiled to let him know she was joking.

"Yeah, I know. You said."

Jonathan lifted the Hardanger as gently as if it were a newborn and slowly ran his palm across its body. The big hands and the gentle caress reminded Marrielle of the man who gave her the fiddle.

"For a moment JC I could have sworn that was Moe Stordhal standing there holding my fiddle."

"Eh? Moe who?"

THE ART OF BEING ONE

Christiana, Copenhagen 10 years earlier

It was the Hardanger fiddle that changed Marrielle's life. Well, Moe Stordhal actually, because if it wasn't for Moe she would never have met Halmund Bjørgum, the Elvis Presley of the Hardanger fiddle.

You could do things in Christiana that weren't tolerated in other parts of Copenhagen. It was a place that attracted bohemians, activists and various waifs and strays from across the world. Not that Moe was any of these. He was simply a hopeless Norwegian romantic, who had moved to Christiana to escape the cold and the dark of the Arctic Circle, and then like ex-pats the world over he would sit pining for the very things he had left behind.

The big place for ex-pats was a little café called Narvic Bar & Grill. It catered largely for the Norwegian contingent with their freshly baked Grovbrod and specialist dishes like Rakfisk, a kind of fermented trout that stank the whole place out when it was on the menu.

The Norsk were as dry as salt cod, but it was a humour that Marrielle had tuned in to and she enjoyed listening to their folk tales and stories of life above the Arctic Circle, as they sat passing around a joint over reindeer, moose sausages and beer.

Most of all she loved the Saturday morning session in Narvic Bar & Grill. It was a long slow morning with the Norwegian crowd straggling in from 10.00am onwards, declaring their allegiance to their country by consuming Grovbrod, Jarlsberg Cheese, and anything else as long as it had a red flag with a black cross on it.

Some of the hipster Norwegian women had started an

embroidery circle and had a small library of patterns, traditional designs from the various homelands of Norway, many going back hundreds of years. It somehow connected them with a land that they were anxious to leave, yet somehow rooted to on the inside. Marrielle embroidered and listened with delight.

Just before 11am, Eric the owner of Narvic Bar & Grill, took part in what had become a Saturday morning ritual. It all started with Moe Stordhal, who had left his family's fishing business in Tromso for what his father considered a life of decadence in Denmark. Moe loved his new life, but after a roll up and a few beers he could become quite melancholy. Homesick almost.

Eric who was very much into rock music, always made sure that Narvic Bar & Grill had a most eclectic mix playing - from The Rolling Stones to The Eagles, Jimi Hendrix and even the occasional bit of Abba. One Saturday morning, Moe began to tell a simple story of how he and his father would always spend their Saturday mornings mending the fishing nets and listening to his father's favourite radio show, Folkets o Busk. It was not a spectacular story, but something about it seemed to trap Moe somewhere in that space between nostalgia and guilt. His eyes moistened and a long and theatrical but good natured negotiation took place between Eric and Moe, with Moe insisting that Eric, just this one time, replace Rod Stewart and tune into Folkets o Busk.

The breakfast group sat enjoying the banter between the two, some supporting Eric, others calling for Moe's wishes to prevail, when one of the embroidery women put down her cushion and needles, and began to clap until the other women joined in and a chant started "Folkets-o-Busk . . . Folkets-o-Busk."

THE ART OF BEING ONE

Reluctantly, Eric agreed to try to tune in to Folkets o Busk and Moe returned to the table to triumphant cheers, before going behind the counter to help Eric locate the right wavelength. Moe turned up the volume and Narvic was flooded with a raucous reel of country fiddles.

Moe took his beer bottle and sat with the embroidery group, watching the ebb and flow of their needles as if he was watching his father mending the nets at home. Folkets o Busk was now playing a kind of fiddle music that Marrielle had never experienced before. It was slow and had a haunting sound almost as if the fiddle was crying out for help. It was sad yet beautiful and Marrielle wiped away a small tear that had welled up in her eye. Moe squeezed her hand and allowed his own tears to trickle down his cheeks uninterrupted.

From that moment Eric had no choice. Saturday mornings at 11am were sacrosanct and Moe had taken it upon himself to lead the Folkets o Busk chant two minutes before tuning in.

After a few weeks, Moe had taken to sitting with the embroidery group during Folkets o Busk. He enjoyed showing his knowledge of Norwegian folk music in between the tunes, and to be fair, he was a mine of inside information. Marrielle loved to hear his tales of the fiddlers.

When it was the one-year anniversary of Narvic's first Folkets o Busk broadcast Moe had decided that this had to be a celebration. By now he didn't need to persuade anyone, even Eric promised to fly in some hjemmebrent brewed by some friends he had in Nordkapp. Moe spent the Friday afternoon fitting his own larger, more powerful speakers to Eric's stereo tuner, and much of Saturday morning adorning Narvic with flags representing each of the Norwegian homelands.

Moe made a short speech in advance of the broadcast, inviting Eric to come out from behind the bar and to receive a round of applause for having the good sense to listen to his suggestion one year earlier. Then Moe surprised everyone by delivering an announcement in the grand style of a showbiz presenter, "Now, I am going to invite you Eric to lead the one year anniversary Folkets o Busk chant . . . take it away Eric."

Eric, delightedly led the chant, whilst Moe went behind the bar and tuned in. There were loud cheers and a standing ovation for Eric as he and Moe danced arm in arm like two love-struck Romeos, to rhythmic clapping and foot stamping.

When the broadcast was over Moe stood to make his second speech of the day. "Marrielle has patiently sat for the best part of a year listening to me blathering on about Norsk music and folklore . . ."

She beamed a smile at him "Moe. You know I've loved every minute of it, you are a wonderful storyteller." At which point there were mock cheers from the group.

Moe continued "In honour of the first anniversary of . . ." He raised his arms and everyone chanted "Folkets o Busk" and to mark Marrielle's talent as a musician and her extreme patience, I would like to present her with a genuine Hardanger fiddle, and my wish is that in one year's time, Marrielle, you are able to play it at the second anniversary of . . . Folkets o Busk."

There were cheers and applause as Eric brought a fiddle case over to Moe and Moe laid it on a table in front of Marrielle as if he were handling a newborn.

It was a fiddle so beautiful, it looked like it had been embroidered, with inlay patterns all along the neck and lacework around the edge of the body. Each of the four strings had a tiny string just below it giving it that crying, ringing sound that could reduce a grown man to tears.

Marrielle held the fiddle, and ran her fingers across each of the pieces of inlay and along the lace work of the body.

For Marrielle. That was the beginning.

The beginning of the art of being one.

Marrielle gently prized the fiddle from Jonathan's hands and polished it with a small embroidered handkerchief.

"And so Mr Goalkeeper ... lumberjack ... whatever you are, that's how I came to be the owner such a beautiful fiddle. Then I went to Norway and become an apprentice to Halmund Bjørgum himself."

She laughed, "Moe says that I play sweeter than Halmund Bjørgum, but that's impossible. Nobody can play sweeter than Halmund."

"That's a nice story. I had a map of Denmark when I was a kid" he said trying to find some way to contribute to the conversation.

"Did you ever go there?"

"Yes a couple of times."

"And? What did you think of my beautiful country?"

He stared at the sky for a moment deep in thought.

"It was just the same as every other place we went to. Airport, hotel room, football stadium, airport. That's what we did everywhere. I've never really seen any of the places

I've been to. I've just got pictures in my head of how I imagined them as a kid when I used to collect maps."

Now it was his turn to tell a tale. He told her of his collection of second hand maps, the tracing paper route from Calgary to Saskatewen that he kept in the back of his exercise book and the airplane ticket from his imaginary dad that never arrived.

She watched as a small tear ran down his cheek and dinked as it dropped onto a fiddle string.

"That sounded like an 'F sharp'" she said.

CHAPTER ELEVEN
KILL OR BE KILLED

"Oh Roberto, that journalist called, you know the one, Brian Dugdale."

Kelly Henry the club's PR, read from a yellow Post-it Note as she walked the manager towards the boardroom.

"You mean the obese imbecile that asks the stupid questions?"

"Say's he's got some information on Christie and wants to meet up."

"Tell him he can have an exclusive interview . . . when he loses twenty kilos."

When Capriolo entered the boardroom, he was surprised at the number of empty chairs. The long mahogany table curved at both ends and could seat twenty-two people, yet only one seat was occupied. Peter Nastasi, the pin stripe suited MBA that the owner had installed as Chief Executive, after growing impatient with the progress made by what he referred to as 'ex-footballers promoted way beyond their level of competence'.

Capriolo and Nastasi, a New Yorker with Italian grandparents, got along well on a personal basis. They had had a few run-ins over recent years as Nastasi tried to apply a little too much business science to 'the project'. They argued over playing budgets which is quite natural, the manager always wants a little bit more, an extra player or two. Their biggest clashes were about how to decide which players to try to buy during the transfer windows. Capriolo argued that he had a gift, an ability to see something in a player which others didn't notice, something that no amount of analysis could describe. He found himself having to justify his well-proven 'God given' gift to Nastasi, a kid out of business school.

Nastasi wanted to buy players based on his *Playing Resource Acquisition Model* (PRAM) with its Lifecycle Costing Framework, Multi-Criteria Options Appraisal and Future Performance Factor Analysis. A compromise was reached whereby Capriolo would be allowed to bring in two wildcards, players who fell slightly outside the normative parameters of PRAM. The following year this would fall to one player and after the third year all acquisitions must be within the acceptable parameters of PRAM.

Capriolo's two wildcards had been the Uruguayan pair Fanni and Mushi. They'd been through the South American youth ranks together since they were twelve, and went as a pair to play in Eredivisie in Holland for a season. Capriolo felt that he had seen something in them. Something he found hard to describe and wanted them on board before they became hot property.

Fanni and Mushi were doing the business on the field. Capriolo was always delighted when any of his players performed well, but even he had to admit to himself that he had never felt such delight as when Fanni or Mushi, or sometimes both, scored a goal. It was a level of elation he had not known before. It was about more than the game, more than the season, more even than the project. It had that added spice. It was Roberto Capriolo's genius versus the cold calculations of PRAM.

"I've briefed the owner about 'the incident' Roberto. I had no choice after Christie disappeared" Natasi said, fiddling with the knobs on the video conferencing console.

"There was no need. I dealt with everything. Fanni and Mushi are family. Christie is nobody. Is simple."

"I don't think the owner quite sees it that way Roberto."

There was a series of bleeps from the teleconference control pad and Kelly clicked 'accept'. The head and shoulders of the owner, Irving Friedel, appeared against a backdrop of New York skyscrapers. Pleasantries were exchanged, but not for long.

"Okay. Let's get down to it" said Friedel "This is a serious situation. We've got the flotation on the Hong Kong Stock Exchange being finalized as we speak. We can't afford to look as though we are not in control. The way it looks to me is that you guys are not in control. I want to know what the Hell's going on. I want it straight and I want it now."

Nastasi turned to Capriolo hoping to deflect the onus for the lack of control "Roberto, I've obviously briefed Mr Friedel based on my earlier talks with everybody involved. Why don't you go over the situation as you saw it?"

Capriolo sat up in his chair and went into his calm, charming mode "Mr Friedel. Is football. Men together all the time, all with a lot of, you know, testosterone. Is inevitable that sometimes there are clashes. Most times they sort themselves out. When they don't we sort them out. That is what we will do with this one."

Friedel's brow furrowed as Capriolo prepared to continue with his gentle sing-song assurances. He stopped him in his tracks.

"That's exactly what you're not doing Roberto. Nobody knows where Christie is and what he's going to say to the press. If what Peter tells me is true this could kill us. It could kill the flotation, which means your Champion's League budget goes out of the window, our debts will be called in and you'll be in charge of a fire sale. In fact you won't be in charge of a fire sale because if we don't sort this out you won't be here. You'll never work again. I'll see to that. Now tell it straight. What happened last week?"

Capriolo swallowed hard and inched up in his chair.

"Is like this. It was after training. Fanni and Mushi they are good boys. Sometimes they stay late, long after the other players have gone home. They like to do extra work on free kicks, perfect those fancy little flicks they like to do. Always together, like two brothers. I like this."

"Okay. That was a great advert for your wildcard signings. Now what happened?" Friedel said banging the table.

THE ART OF BEING ONE

"So it was late everybody else had gone and Little Roberto and I were walking past the changing rooms. We hear banging about, shouting as if there is a fight. When we go in Mushi has Christie bent over in a headlock and Fanni is behind him gripping his body. Christie has blood pouring from his nose."

"Cut to the chase Roberto. Christie says they attempted a sexual assault. Are these two wildcards faggots?"

"I hear him say this. The way I see it and Little Roberto is witness also, is what I call horseplay."

"Horseshit Roberto. Christie could be giving a statement to the police now. We've lost control of the situation that seems to be the bottom line."

Nastasi referred to the briefing paper he had emailed to Friedel.

"As you can see, if Christie makes a complaint, all three would be suspended during an investigation. As a result maybe we don't make The Champion's League and the flotation is cancelled. With all of the knock-on effects this could cost us £600 million. We could go into meltdown."

Capriolo saw this as his chance to demonstrate to Friedel that he was in control "After he make the . . . the allegation . . . I take him in my office. I calm him, clean up his nose bleed. I tell him about my life. How I grew up in a small town in Le Marche called Jesi . . . it means Jesus. We are the special people, the people of Jesus. We grow up with a mantra *Il morta es l'autres il vita* . . . at some time in our lives we all pledge to do this. It is a kind of metaphor. I say to Jonathan this is his time, for the team, the family, the project. I mean it metaphorically, I say Jonathan, it is your time. You must die so that others may live. I mean he have to sacrifice himself with this 'sexual assault' thing. For the team."

"And what did he say?" Friedel said with a slight mocking tone.

"He calmed. He's an intelligent, sensitive boy. He say he would go home and think about if he should die so others may live. That was it. Next thing we know he is walking off the pitch."

"I'll tell you a little story about me" Friedel said moving closer to the microphone "I grew up in The Bronx. We have a little mantra too. 'Kill or be killed'. You got that Roberto? 'Kill or be killed'. Now kill this situation dead. Go get Christie and bring him back in."

CHAPTER TWELVE
OH MY DARLING

As Jonathan and Marrielle emerged from a clearing in the forest, a woman in red Hunter wellingtons and an unfeasibly neat Barbour jacket lifted the hatchback of her small Volvo compact to release an excited schnauzer. It ran in small circles around the Epping Forest visitors' car park, before lifting its leg and leaving its calling card on the front tyre of an orange and white VW camper van with its box-like concertina roof raised.

"He did that yesterday" Marrielle shouted towards the Barbour woman, who in turn, remonstrated with the dog, wagging her finger as she clipped on his lead.

"I'm so sorry. He's such a naughty boy aren't you?" followed by what sounded like subdued baby talk.

"Don't worry Clementine will understand. She's a nature girl."

Barbour woman smiled and slipped into the forest still talking to the dog in their secret language.

"Who's Clementine?" asked Jonathan.

Marrielle smiled and played the gracious hostess. "Clementine I would like you to meet my new friend JC." She made a grand sweeping gesture with her arm towards the van, "JC. This is Clementine. My inspiration, my home and of course my darling."

He looked at the van, then at Marrielle, then again at the van. "You live in that? You're kidding."

"Ssshhh. She's very sensitive" Marrielle lowered her voice to a whisper "You have to call her Clementine, for heaven's sake don't say 'that' or worse still 'it' otherwise she tends to have a bit of a breakdown just when you don't need it. And yes this is where I live. Clementine and I are members of the small home appreciation society. If you ask nicely she will make you a cup of tea."

Marrielle slid open the side door of the VW to reveal her home.

Soft sheepskin throws covered the 'rock & roll' bed, which, with a rock and a roll and the click of a catch, could convert a bench seat into a boudoir. There were brightly embroidered scatter cushions in Norsk tradition with pinks, yellows, browns and gold, which stood out against the white of the throw as if she had planted a little indoor garden in the snow. Small pictures and mottos were scattered around, glued to cupboard doors or hanging from little white plastic hooks. She swung open a cupboard door and laid it flat to deliver up a two-ring gas cooker, pulled out an orange triangular kettle and with a scratch, a hiss and a whiff of calor gas, ignited the flame below it.

THE ART OF BEING ONE

Jonathan squeezed himself next to Marrielle on the bench seat, a big man in a small space. His shoulders turned from side to side as he surveyed the tiny domestic scene. A small rectangular piece of cloth hung from a cupboard door. He read out loud the words that Marrielle had embroidered.

"Draw your life in pencil – Halmund"

"Ah you like that eh?" Marrielle said, as she leaned across to pull two cups from a small cupboard.

"I don't get it"

"You will. Tea or coffee?"

"And what does 'Halmund' mean?

"Have you forgotten what I told you already? In the forest?

Marrielle had practiced on Moe Stordhal's Hardanger fiddle for only nine months before she made her first public appearance. She was a natural musician anyway and her nimble fingers danced across the fretwork of the Hardanger with an ease that seemed somehow unnatural for someone so young.

It was Moe Stordahl's birthday, a Thursday evening, and a small crowd began to assemble in The Narvic Bar & Grill. It was not an organized party as such. Eric produced a small pale yellow blotkake, layers of cream and berries between sponge and covered in marzipan, with six candles and placed it on one of the worn pine tables, before turning towards Moe and his group who were standing around the bar area.

English was the predominant language spoken in Narvic,

but in a tongue in cheek nod to Moe, Eric clapped his hands and shouted "God Kveld mein damer og herrer." This got the attention of Moe and his little group, and Moe saw in between the heads of the others the flickering flames of the candles on Eric's small cake.

"Moe, I invite you to come and blow out the candles." There was a cheer and Moe made towards the cake before Eric stopped the noise by raising his hands "Stop. Stop. It is important that Moe understands why there are six candles on the cake . . ." he paused for dramatic effect, looking around the room as if reaching for some profound explanation, before breaking into laughter and exclaiming "There is one for every twenty years of your life."

Moe moved forward amidst peels of laughter and grabbed Eric in a gentle, playful headlock. He blew out the candles, still with Eric's head in his arm "Even if I was one hundred and twenty Eric, I could whoop your arse and still blow out my birthday candles." He released Eric and grabbed him in a bear hug and the two stood with their arms around each other's shoulders as pieces of cake were sliced and handed around, for a moment calling a truce on the banter which had become their stock in trade.

Then Moe's body seemed to freeze as if someone had tipped an icicle down the collar of his shirt, as a high pitched, intricate plucking of strings came from the direction of the front door, before Marrielle launched into Klunkarren Neri Neset Minne, one of Moe's folk favourites.

As Moe turned to look, Eric pushed a chair into the back of his legs and Moe sat open mouthed watching Marrielle lost in the music that he so loved. It was impossible from the first couple of bars for him not to be overcome by emotion and he became lost in a nether world somewhere between Narvic and a Norway that probably never existed as the tears just kept on coming, and Moe just allowed them to flow.

Marrielle drew the bow across the bridge for a final long, haunting peel and then made five or six gentle plucks of the neck strings that sounded like the distant peeling of the bells in Tromso Cathedral before the fiddle fell silent.

There was no applause. Everybody looked towards Moe who sat tearstained and motionless for a moment, they awaited his verdict. He slowly rose from the chair staring intensely into Marielle's eyes "That was sweeter than Halmund Bjørgum" he said as he crossed the floor and held Marrielle in a hug so tight that she had to gulp for air, as Narvic rocked with loud applause.

Eric and Moe rooted out an old Dansette cassette tape recorder and began setting it up in a far corner of Narvic. The ancient machine was battered and held together with some green vinyl tape, and they became lost in their joint endeavor, as they fiddled with the stick microphone and ran a series of sound checks.

When they were ready, Moe insisted that everyone be seated and pleaded for silence as he positioned Marielle in front of the microphone, moving her a few inches this way, then back a bit as if somehow he knew what he was doing. He returned to his seat and looked over to Eric who was crouched by the battered Dansette with three fingers at the ready waiting for Moe's signal. Eric clicked three buttons down simultaneously, Moe, about to prompt Marrielle to begin playing, suddenly began making a cutthroat gesture towards her and rolling his eyes. He quietly tiptoed over to the microphone and leaned in towards it. His mouth made an almost perfect circle as he sucked in some air to make the sound of the Norwegian gluttlestop, as if to emphasise the importance of what he was about to say "Hooooh. This is Marrielle Lindstrom performing Klunkarren Neri Neset Minne . . . live." He stayed crouched as he tiptoed back to his seat, catching a glare from Eric who was still crouched by the Dansette. Quickly Moe, swiveled and leaned back into the microphone adding "Live . . . from Eric Hulvars Narvic Bar & Grill, Chritiana." Eric tipped Moe an appreciative wink as he slipped back into his seat and the room fell silent as Marrielle repeated her performance.

It was some months later that Moe came clattering through the doors of Narvic carrying a clunky black box that was his telephone answering machine. He seemed in a slight panic and a little breathless as he banged the contraption onto the bar.

"Where have you been?" Eric smiled looking down at what must have been one of the first answering machines in Denmark 'The museum for failed products'?"

Moe was about to respond when he remembered why he had lumbered this thing across to Narvic. "Hush Eric. Let's plug this in. I want you to hear this." He turned to three of the regulars who were on high stools by the bar "Karl, everybody come over and listen to this."

They all moved over and huddled around Moe. Eric plugged in the machine, rewound and pressed the 'play' button.

'Beep'. "Hello to you Mister Moe Stordahl, this is Halmund Bjørgum here" Moe elbowed the people closest to him at the bar, pointed to the answer machine and silently mouthed the name 'Halmund Bjørgum' with an astonished look on his face. Eric raised his eyebrows slightly impressed that the Elvis Presley

of the Hardanger Fiddle had contacted Moe. "I'm sorry to have taken so long to respond to your letter with the tape. I was busy and forgot about it. Only today as I sat with the family preparing for Christmas did I play it. I can tell right away that this girl has a special talent. I only ever take one apprentice at one time. I have a vacancy if she would like to be the one. Have a Merry Christmas Mr Moe Stordhal."

The group at the bar made a few encouraging noises, nodded heads and gave Moe the odd congratulatory slap on the shoulder before returning to their high stools by the bar, where one of the group spoke in German "What's he been taking?" bringing hoots of laughter from the others.

Eric poured a beer for Moe and placed it on the counter "Here Moe, drink this and come back down to earth."

Moe looked star struck "Did you hear that Eric? 'Have a Merry Christmas Mr Moe Stordhal'. That was 'the' Halmund Bjørgum talking to me."

Eric busied himself drying some glasses. He gave a mischievous smile "I don't want to rain on your parade Moe", which of course he did "But he was speaking to your ancient answering machine." Eric disappeared into the back room.

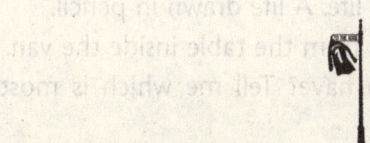

"I spent five years with Halmund" Marrielle said switching off the gas jet underneath the kettle.

"Oh I'm sorry it didn't work out" Jonathan flushed.

Marrielle laughed hysterically. Jonathan flushed even more

deeply and squirmed uncomfortably. She gripped the top of his hand.

"That's hilarious."

"I don't get it" he said.

His discomfort made him feel as if the small confines of the van were closing in on him and he clumsily slid out of the seat into the car park where he made small circular movements like the Schnauzer.

Marrielle laughed even harder.

"Look. I'd better get going" he said.

"No" she slid out of the side door of the van and steadied his nervous flitting about by holding both of his hands.

"Stay and have some tea. Please. It's just that what you said about Halmund was funny that's all."

Halmund had been her mentor. After Moe sent the tape, she went to Norway to be his apprentice. In the summer she would earn a living playing weddings, fetes and festivals. In the winter, Halmund taught her to make silver jewellery. The nimble fingers of the fiddle player were ideally suited to the intricate shaping and engraving of precious metals.

"Halmund taught me how to play, how to earn a living, but most of all how to live a life. A life drawn in pencil."

She grabbed the two cups from the table inside the van.

"Now which cup will you have? Tell me which is most suited to your personality."

She proffered the first mug. It had a picture of a sunflower and a legend as if someone had drawn the words freehand *Just one small sunflower would make me really happy.*

He looked puzzled. "How can a sunflower make you happy?"

"Perhaps you are this one then." She proffered the second cup which had a jumble of multi-coloured writing *Sometimes I pretend to be normal, but it gets boring, so I just go back to being me.*

He stared from cup to cup, the swirling sound of the Upton Park crowd seeped into his head "I'm forever blowing bubbles/ pretty bubbles in the air . . .." He was looking down on himself drifting out of his penalty area, watching the number 1 on the back of his shirt disappear down the players tunnel.

"JC? JC? You just have to choose one cup or the other. It's not a test. JC? Are you awake?"

His eyes widened and he jolted. "Yes. Yes that's me. Sometimes I pretend to be normal. I'll have my cuppa in that one."

They leaned against the front of Clementine sipping tea and swapping stories, though Jonathan had to admit that his best stories were just the ones he had made up as a kid.

"I'd always loved the sound of Reykjavic" he volunteered. "That was one of my favourite names when I was a kid. I always wanted to go there. We went for a qualifying game once."

"What was it like? Don't tell me - airport, hotel room, football stadium, airport?"

He caught her eye and they laughed simultaneously.

"You're not as daft as you look Marrielle."

"Thank you I take that as a compliment. And you, Mr Lumberjack goalkeeper. You are not as scary as you look" she held out her cup "Salut, Big Hands. Shall we have a proper drink?"

She opened a bottle of Aquavit and produced two small shot glasses.

"I thought we would have one for the road. Aquavit, the water of life as they say" she poured a shot and handed it to him.

He sniffed the clear liquid and stared into it. "I don't really drink. The gaffer prefers it if we don't."

She stuck out her bottom lip "But that was in your old life. I thought you were drawing a new one?"

"Yeah. Here's to whathisname . . . Halmund" he downed the shot, wheezed and spun round in a circle on his heel.

Marrielle followed suit and banged her glass on the camper van table. "You like that? One for the road eh? She offered to top up his glass.

He wiped the back of his hand across his mouth "I'll be okay with that one thanks."

"Come on, man up goalkeeper. Let's have one for the road. Where are you going from here anyway?"

"I suppose I should start to head for home" he smiled nervously "I'll have to face the music sometime."

"Where's home goalkeeper?"

"Up North" he said, suddenly flipping into flatter vowel sounds, the way he'd spoken when he was a child. "Where will you go?"

"I just go where Clementine tells me to go. She has a compass." She walked around the van, opened the driver's side door and leaned in, tapping the compass with her index finger and making "Aha" sounds like a doctor trying to diagnose a chest infection.

She walked back around the van.

"Well, Clementine's compass says north, so I guess we are going Ooooop North. Want a lift?"

CHAPTER THIRTEEN
CAFÉ VINCENZO

Vincenzo's Italian café was an anomaly amongst the glitzy glass and chrome eateries that dominated the strip that was Alderley Edge. It had become hemmed in by ever advancing beauty salons, estate agents selling the dream and designer shops with WAG sized price tags. In the overall pecking order, Vincenzo's was on a par with the Cancer Research Charity Shop, and probably not as glamorous as The Oxfam Book Shop. Defying all commercial logic, it stood small and stubborn, like some long forgotten outpost of the Italian Empire.

Vincenzo was a one-man band, he cooked his simple Northern Italian food, waited his seven tables and cleaned what needed to be cleaned. A grey haired aging eccentric from Trieste, resisting invasions was in his genes, and somehow he had managed to resist the march of gentrification that had rapidly overtaken what locals still liked to call 'The Village'.

He chose his customers, they didn't choose him. He was a master of the well-turned insult if he didn't like the cut of a customer's jib. He didn't seem to care one way or the other whether people spent money or not. If all else failed he kept in his pocket seven laminated slips, each saying 'Reserved', and he would systematically place these, one on each empty table, and turn to the unwelcome customers with a shrug and a "Sorry we is full."

The place had become a home from home for Roberto Capriolo and his entourage - Marco, Giovanni, Paolo, Little Roberto, Fredo and various other backroom staff or visiting family members. When they arrived Vincenzo would put reserved signs on all the other tables whilst encouraging any existing customers to leave, before putting a chair across the door. In his small white chef's hat and white overalls he would wait on the Capriolo crew with feigned indifference, whilst keeping an eye out for Paparazzi.

With Capriolo seated at his table and in full flow, Vincenzo pushed his hip against his shoulder knocking him slightly sideways and unceremoniously banged down two large bowls containing Penne Arrabbiata.

"Prego."

Little Roberto, Fredo and Giovanni exchanged nervous glances at the sight of Capriolo being pushed around, fearing an explosion of anger, but he just turned and thanked Vincenzo, then turned to the table, held out his hands and gave permission to eat.

"Mangiare."

Fredo sat wide eyed as if awaiting an eruption from his boss.

"What? Why you look like this? This is his domain. He is boss here. What he say goes. Now mangiare."

There was a babble of animated conversation accompanied by much hand waving, squeezing of arms and grabbing of shoulders. Views were exchanged on everything from the future of Southern Italy, now that it had broken off from the North and become a German dependency, to the takeover of Glasgow Rangers by an Italian Ice Cream manufacturer.

As Vincenzo began to clear the table Capriolo asked him to lock the door and leaned forward, gesturing his group to do likewise. He placed a finger over his lips and then began speaking in hushed tones.

"I know we say we never mention Jonathan again. That is for the players. It's important that we sort this out quickly. So what do we know about him?"

Capriolo looked around the table. There was a series of shrugs and glances, each person hoping that someone else would come up with something. Fredo broke the silence.

"I know he lives local. I see him only once though, going into the library."

Giovanni lurched back in his chair and prodded his hands forward with disdain.

"The library?" he said with disgust.

"Yes. He say that he like the smell and the feel of books."

There was a silence. Paulo coughed nervously and looked down at the table.

Marco fidgeted with a napkin and spluttered before he spoke.

"The smell and feel of books? Isn't that a little . . . a bit . . . you know . . . a bit suspect?"

Paulo screwed up his napkin and threw it down on the table.

"Pfffff. Is not normal. Once before a game I think he is staring at me. He say he is staring at the coatpeg. He says he do this since he was a little boy. Now I begin to wonder. The smell and the feel of books? Uggh. It make my flesh creep."

"Maybe he stare at you because he like you Paulo" interjected Little Roberto puckering up his lips and blowing a kiss across the table.

There was a burst of laughter and Paulo had to be restrained from leaving his seat as he tried to remonstrate with Little Roberto. When order was restored Paulo directed a look of disgust across the table. Little Roberto mirrored his daggers, and the two locked eyes for a few moments.

Capriolo took over again.

"For me he seems like a nice boy, but lately I hear a few whispers about him. There has been a suggestion that maybe, just maybe, he drives on the other side of the autostrade. What do you think Paulo."

Paulo flushed a little "Why are you asking me? For me that's it. I never shower with him again. Even if he come back."

Little Roberto, nudged the elbow of Marco who was sitting next to him and then addressed Paulo deadpan like a weary doctor checking for symptoms.

"But you shower with him before, yes?"

Paulo jumped out of his seat smashing his chair hard against Vincenzo's refrigerated counter, leant across the table and grabbed Little Roberto by the scarf which tightened like a noose around his neck, causing him to gulp for air. Vincenzo joined the others in a ritual restraint of Paulo, who was eventually persuaded to calm down, but not before he had issued the regulation number of curses in the direction of Little Roberto.

"You stop this. What did I say to you and to the players? They are trying to break us with this Jonathan thing. We have to stay together, not this fighting. We need to get Christie back quickly. Is better. We make things smooth again. Jonathan he will see sense. If not we have to destroy him. Is simple."

Fredo looked puzzled "But boss, how we destroy him? We don't even know where he is."

"I think it was our fellow countryman Verdi who said that 'The pen is mightier than the sword', Fredo my friend." Paulo looked agitated. "What is the matter Paulo?"

"Shakespeare. It was Shakespeare boss. Shakespeare said that" Paulo said sheepishly before quickly glancing towards Little Roberto and then looking down at his crumpled napkin.

"Ah . . . Ok . . . Shakespeare."

Capriolo appeared taken aback as he eyed Paulo suspiciously.

"You are an enigma Paulo. You surprise me every day. A man who despises books, but knows his Shakespeare. Mmmm. As I say, an enigma."

Marco elbowed Little Roberto and whispered.

"What does enigma mean?"

Little Roberto gave a knowing look, nodded and muttered a little bit too loudly "A bit suspect."

There was a tapping on the glass door panel, which caused Vincenzo to run around from behind his refrigerated cabinet and begin shouting.

"Closed. We are closed. No more" he wagged his hand several times across his neck in a cutthroat gesture.

Capriolo stood up.

"No. No. Vincenzo, it is Kelly. She is one of us. Please. Let her in."

Kelly Henry, for all her slick black business suit and severe but chic chignon looked a little flustered as Vincenzo opened a small crack in the door and beckoned her in with a nod and a snarl as if he were the doorman at an underground Soho nightclub.

"Sit down Kelly, the boys are just leaving."

There was a noisy melee of goodbyes and hellos with the group in turn hugging Vincenzo and kissing Kelly when Little Roberto crashed between two stainless steel chairs and onto the hard tile floor, knocking his head against the skirting. Paulo held up his hands in innocence as everybody turned to him.

"What? It was an accident. He fell over."

Capriolo flipped "What I just tell you? Ha? You drive me crazy with this infighting. No more, you hear? Now go."

Kelly moved aside an empty pasta bowl and laid her notebook on the table. "Well, this is a . . . a quaint . . . sort of place"

Capriolo tutted. "Is a dump. We like Vincenzo. That's all."

"Ah Vincenzo is Italian too, is he?" she said, trying to lighten the tension.

"Trieste. It was fought over many times. Sometimes it was in Italy, sometimes it was not. So he is fifty-fifty, eh Vincenzo?"

Vincenzo stopped sweeping the floor for a moment, held

the top of the broom handle against the underside of his chin and thought for a few seconds.

"Fifty-fifty? Maybe you should ask Paulo that one."

Vincenzo turned and resumed his sweeping.

Capriolo was poised to laugh and then stopped and drew back for a moment trying to decipher what Vincenzo meant 'Paulo?' he thought 'Paulo is from Trieste? No. I know he is from Milan . . . what?' he put his elbow on the table and his chin on his hand, lost in thought for a moment.

Kelly interrupted his pondering. "Roberto, shall we . . . ?"

"Ah yes, sorry, I was just thinking about things. Now, we are meeting the fat journalist, Brian isn't it?"

Kelly produced a small thin paper file from her bag and placed it on the table. It contained a few loose sheets of paper, on top of which, was a hand written note torn from a message pad.

"He left me a message. It was on my desk when I got in" she said, hoping to distance herself from any impending tirade of anger. 'Kelly. Had a call from a Mr Dugdale. Says he and his business manager have been unavoidably delayed due to traffic problems of some sort. He was a bit vague. Would like to rearrange for tomorrow' She shrugged and put on a look of frustration "That's all I've got."

Capriolo looked puzzled "What he mean 'business manager'? Since when did journalists have business managers?"

"Apparently, he's left the paper. He reckons that he's some sort of freelance investigative journalist now."

"Investigative? Like a kind of detective you mean? Maybe that's what we need. Anyway I want you to handle the press. I'm putting Paulo in charge of the team for the next match.

I'm going to finish this Christie affair myself. Quickly."

Kelly placed her palms on the table "I'm not sure that's wise Roberto, how's that going to look with everything that's gone on lately?"

"Kelly, everything is at stake for me. I learn early that the one person who can do most to change what happens to me, is me. I will do it. I find Jonathan, I bring him back, we make it smooth. You tell the press I'm on a scouting mission – looking for a player – he just happens to be our own player. You don't have to tell them that last bit."

When the PR agenda was concluded, Kelly entered what felt like an uncomfortable negotiation with Vincenzo about unlocking the door whilst Capriolo remained seated in silence for some time before he settled his bill, shook Vincenzo's hand and gave him a hug. He opened the door to leave, stopped and then closed it again turning to face Vincenzo.

"Vincenzo. Tell me. Paulo. Tell me he is not driving on the other side of the autostrade."

Vincenzo picked up his broom, turned his back on Capriolo and began sweeping the floor. Then he stopped and spoke without turning around "You like Shakespeare Mr Capriolo? Go look up Hamlet. There is a scene where he is in the theatre with the Queen. That will tell you all you need to know."

Capriolo looked puzzled and waited for an explanation, but Vincenzo continued with his sweeping.

As the door slammed closed, Vincenzo stopped sweeping and smiled to himself "Oh, and Mr Capriolo, Just make sure you don't look it up in the library."

CHAPTER FOURTEEN
TO THE EDGE

As Marrielle bobbed and weaved Clementine along one 'B' road after another, Jonathan gazed out at the countryside. He'd never looked closely at hedgerows before and he found himself marvelling at the beauty of hawthorn, neatly trimmed, its square solid shape softened by bursts of delicate white flower.

It had been some time since either he or Marrielle had spoken, yet he felt comfortable in the silence, lost in his thoughts and feeling under no pressure to do anything or say anything. Every field seemed to offer something of interest. He found he enjoyed following the tracks of tractor tyres that weaved through rows of early crops and then turned back on themselves as they reached a field boundary.

Eventually he broke the silence. "How long before we hit the motorway?" he said.

Marrielle exaggerated a puzzled look "Why would we want to hit the motorway?"

"It's quicker isn't it?"

"Are you in a hurry?"

He thought for a moment "Er . . . no."

"Then the journey is the important thing. The destination will take care of itself."

He nodded and wished that he had thought of that. His eyes ran along the dashboard until he fixed his gaze on the compass that had been attached with two small screws. He watched as it swirled gently around mirroring the curves in the road and he decided that he liked something about the dependability of the compass needle. A bit like the goalkeeper standing solid in the swirling ebb and flow of a hotly contested match.

"I've been watching that compass" he nodded towards it as if it were a slightly threatening dog whose gaze he didn't dare to break.

She smiled "What an exciting life you lead."

"You said that Clementine's compass was pointing to the North and so you would be able to take me with you."

"Yeeeees" she said slowly as if humouring a small child.

"Well I've been watching it and the compass is always pointing to the North."

"Yeeees . . . and so?"

"So you weren't going North, you just said that?"

"My life is drawn in pencil. I believe in serendipity. The art of the happy accident. Perhaps you were a happy accident and you are leading me somewhere. Maybe somewhere important. I don't know, we will find out."

THE ART OF BEING ONE

Jonathan struggled to take this in. His whole life had been about preparation and planning, then reflection to see if anything could have done better. His was a lifetime of concentration on minor details, trying to leave as little to chance as possible.

He would spend hours every week just watching DVD compilations of his opponent's penalty takers, trying to detect a pattern or a preference in their shooting. Looking at the way they stood to see if some small aspect of their body language might give a clue as to which way they might strike the ball.

Then there were the rituals. Always, but always, two poached eggs for breakfast on the day of a game. Never scrambled or fried, they had to be poached. If they were slightly overdone, this would cause him to tense up a little, but he had made a pact with himself that as long as his eggs were poached, everything was going to be all right.

The goalkeeping gloves were another thing. If his team won or drew, he would continue to wear the same goalkeeping gloves for the next match. If the game ended in defeat he never wanted to see those gloves again. In the early days he would cut a seam with a small pair of nail scissors, then make a long tear in one of the fingers, so that he could go to the kit man and ask for a new pair. When eventually the kit man noticed a pattern to the broken seams, they agreed that if Jonathan autographed his losing gloves, they would be dispatched to a local charity, and he could have a new pair.

Serendipity was a foreign country to him. His heart quickened, he became slightly breathless and gripped the dashboard with both hands, before a small shudder of excitement took hold at the thought of not knowing what was going to happen next.

Closing his eyes he imagined himself as a small boy sitting at the kitchen table examining a map of a land called Serendipity with his mother scuttling around in the background. He saw himself quietly whispering the word 'ser-en-dip-ity', and liking the sound of it, taking a soft pencil and drawing a route through a country track, along a mountain pass and then down to the sea. Gently he whispered the name of the coastal settlement 'Christiana'.

He jerked out of a half sleep causing Marrielle to swerve a little whilst he breathlessly fought with the Velcro flap on his pocket, rummaged inside and pulled out his Travelcard. Holding it close to his face he traced the tear stained cross with his index finger.

Gears crunched as Marrielle conquered the swerve then changed down to third to take a tight bend.

"Die so that others may live" he whispered and again traced the cross with his finger.

"JC are you awake?" Marrielle pulled Clementine tight into a small field entrance, barred by a gate and switched off the engine.

"You scared me then. What happened to you?"

"I think I must have nodded off. I used to sleep walk when I was a kid. It was like that. They would sometimes find me at the bottom of the stairs in the children's home talking gibberish."

"So what's with this Travelcard thing?"

He slid the Travelcard back in his pocket, checking the seal on the Velcro flap three times.

"The Travelcard? I don't know. It just somehow makes me feel that everything is going to be alright. Maybe I'll need it to get back."

"Back from where?"

He caught her gaze and smiled.

"That place we are going to. You know. Serendipity."

She smiled back and he laughed until his laughter made her laugh. Then it came like a torrent. Laughter like he had never known before and his eyes filled with tears so that the compass on Clementine's dashboard appeared to be wandering around in a drunken stupor.

When the laughter had subsided Jonathan touched Marrielle's arm apologetically.

"Oh, I forgot to give you something."

He carefully began to unzip his Velcro pocket.

"You're giving me your precious Travelcard? I'm honoured."

"No. I forgot to give you this."

He pulled out the crumpled ten-pound note that Reverend Darren had given him, and laid it flat on the dashboard trying to smooth out the creases.

"It's all I've got on me but you can have it. For petrol and stuff."

Marrielle looked at the creased up note with amusement for a moment "Do you know how much petrol you can buy with ten pounds?"

Jonathan made as if he was going to answer and then stopped himself short. He thought hard trying to do a few mental calculations in his head, then he had to admit to himself that he didn't know the basic numbers – how much it cost to fill up the tank of his car, how many litres it needed, the cost per litre and so on. The price of petrol just didn't register on his radar screen.

"To be honest Marrielle, I have no idea. That sounds really bad doesn't it?"

"Halmund used to say that if you didn't know the price of a litre of petrol you had lost touch with reality."

"Yeah. Maybe that's right. But I can get more money for you, I just have to . . ."

"If I want anything from you JC I will ask. I accept your contribution of ten pounds", she said whipping the note from between his fingers and the dashboard. "I've always thought that money spoils things. You create something of beauty and money steps into the equation and destroys it. I'll take the ten pounds. You keep your money wherever it is that you keep it."

"But what happens when we run out of money?" he asked.

"We won't. Necessity, as they say, is the mother of invention. I can play the fiddle, I'm a silversmith so I can always make something to sell. Besides, people can be very kind. And you? You must have your talents also."

He spread out his fingers and looked at his large hands.

"I've got these. But there are only twenty jobs for goalkeepers in The Premier League and I've just walked out of one of them."

The motorway was not Marrielle's preferred option, but on this journey, it just made a lot more sense to take the odd stretch here and there. Clementine was flashed onto the M6 motorway at Coventry, by a green Eddie Stobart artic, probably bound for the Chelford hub, or possibly heading up as far as Carlisle.

Truckers tended to have a soft spot for anything a bit unusual, and a forty-year old VW with flowers, Norwegian plates and a tall redhead at the wheel tended to brighten up their day. They flashed their lights, honked their horns and best of all, on occasion, come over and have a chat at truck stops.

Quite often they would tell a story of how they had restored an ancient car or motorbike, going into technical details about overhead camshafts and the like, as if Marrielle was some kind of expert. Though she had no idea what they were talking about it created a kind of camaraderie with what she called 'The Trucker Tribe'. They were a tribe that tended to have a little sadness behind their eyes. On the open road but imprisoned by schedules that took them to places like Histon and Crawley.

Her favourite group had been 'The Hitchhiker Tribe'. A random assortment of people going to random places. Hippies; academics; students; world travelers; hungry people; and even homeless people. She'd become adept at sizing them up from a distance. Often she found it was just something in the way that they stood, or small clues on their baggage, that enabled her to slow up slightly as she approached them, then make an instant, intuitive decision about whether to stop and pick them up.

She kept the addresses of people that she had picked up in a small notebook with an embroidered cover that she had made herself. It was a bit 'geeky', but people would always say "Keep in touch" or "Look me up if ever you are in . . .." Once or twice she did. She had danced the Tango with Karl by the river in Berlin and toasted Valpurgis Eve in Upsalla with Daniela, a Colombian student who was on an exchange programme.

Yet the 'Hitchhiker Tribe' had all but become extinct. Lost to a world where twenty-four hour news made us believe that everybody was an axe murderer. Lost to gated communities, security systems, warm plush cars that must be kept clean, low cost airlines, and jet setting gap years. The only remnant seemed to be fat middle-aged men with wispy hair holding up temporary number plates at the exits of service stations.

She missed the days of those random, unexpected conversations. The occasional beer, the odd flirtation, the sense that she and the people that she picked up were heading off to some exciting yet undiscovered future. The sense of connection.

Then hitchhikers just disappeared, seemingly all on the same day, as if the United Nations had passed some global resolution banning them from the sides of roads forever.

At Corley Services, Jonathan strolled onto the grassy verge usually reserved for stretching the little legs of dogs that had been cooped up in cars for far too long, whilst Marrielle used the ladies and picked up a few bits and pieces from the shop.

The London Underground uniform didn't help. With that, his rapidly emerging full-on beard and one of Marrielle's woolen hats with pigtails, he looked like a cross between a Big Issue seller and a Yogi as he began a stretching routine that was an essential part of a goalkeepers everyday life. He held a long stretch despite the unwanted attentions of a small white dog, not much bigger than a large rat, and not much different to look at.

For the first time since the 'incident' as they liked to call it, he allowed the images of Fanni and Mushi to pass through his mind. The struggle. The blood. The lies.

"The bastards" he whispered, "Devious bastards."

He began a series of springing bunny hops, his knees almost touching his chin on the upward thrust. His voice no longer a whisper.

"Well Mr. Capriolo . . . you got what you wanted. I died so that that your devious cheating Uruguayan's could live . . . I hope you're happy with yourself"

He planted his feet on the floor, crouched slightly and began an on-the-spot sprint, banging his feet hard into the ground until, on reaching a point of exhaustion he let out a yell and rolled to the floor.

A nearby woman picked up her black curly haired poodle and pulled him close to her chin, quickly walking away and back to the car.

Calmly he rose to his feet, collected himself and determinedly returned to his routine. He raised his arms and swung them to the left and right, with his legs reeling in the opposite direction, advancing in what looked rather like a slightly subdued version of *Riverdance*.

Marielle crept up behind him carrying a small plastic bag of assorted dried fruits and some fresh orange juice.

"JC" She giggled, "You're a dancer as well? Is there no end to your talents?"

He froze with his body shaped for the opening moment of the sand dance.

"It's called active stretching this is."

"Hmmm, I'm not sure that it will catch on. It needs a bit of fiddle music perhaps."

She smiled broadly to make sure that he knew that she was joking. Relaxing a little he realized that his arms were still locked in the upright position like someone determined to win at Simple Simon. There was a moment of self-consciousness as he became aware that he'd tuned out the dog walkers and the picnickers in the way that he used to tune out the sound of a crowd of 70,000 people. Looking sheepishly at the ground, he felt the outside of his pocket and ran his finger around the perimeter of the Travelcard inside.

Marrielle gestured excitedly.

"Come and see what I've found JC. They're in the van."

She took his arm and walked him in the direction of Clementine.

"You remember I was telling you about the extinction of the hitchhiker? Well I've found a couple, alive and well and heading in the direction of Alderley Edge, which is not too far from where we are headed, right?"

"You've picked up a couple of strangers. Are you mad?"

"Yes, probably. I picked one up a couple of days ago wearing a yellow dayglow jacket and having some kind of perverted love affair with a London Underground Travelcard."

She uncoupled her arm and walked on.

"Whoa. Hold on Marrielle. I didn't mean it like that. I guess I've not quite grasped this serendipity idea yet. Hang on, wait for me."

THE ART OF BEING ONE

As they climbed into Clementine, Marrielle came over all dinner party hostess and began to make formal introductions, the new guests seated on the bench seat some way in the back of the van.

"JC I'd like you to meet Brian and . . . what was it again, Moonboots? I love that."

Moonboots leaned forward and proffered his hand toward Jonathan "Brian, my name's actually Brian as well." They locked fingers by way of a handshake.

Dugdale looked incredulously at Moonboots.

"Brian? Since when were you called Brian?"

"I've always been Brian"

"I've never heard anyone call you Brian. You've always been Moonboots. Everyone knows that. You're Moonboots"

"Sorry to disappoint you Brian, but I was originally known as Brian long before people started calling me Moonboots."

Marrielle interrupted what had all of the hallmarks of a domestic spat "Well, look Moonboots . . . er Brian. To avoid confusion shall we just call you Moonboots for the duration of the journey?"

"That's fine by me. I like Moonboots. Who wants to be called Brian?" he turned to Dugdale and gave him a pitiful look.

Dugdale looked deflated as if he had just discovered that Batman was really married with a couple of kids and living in Balsall Heath.

CHAPTER FIFTEEN

TWO EXTRA BODIES

Clementine was struggling to top forty miles per hour with the weight of two extra bodies on board and it was a slow journey north.

After the initial pleasantries and introductions, there had been a long silence. Not the comfortable silence that Jonathan had enjoyed earlier when he was alone with Marrielle, now it was a kind of silence that made him feel anxious. A silence that he wanted to break, but he was fearful of speaking in case he should give the game away and be recognized.

It was Moonboots who lifted the mood "I couldn't help noticing your number plates. Norwegian if I'm not mistaken. Would I be right in saying Oppland?"

Marrielle looked astounded "Yes. How the Hell did you know that?"

Dugdale looked at Moonboots and shook his head in disbelief.

Moonboots continued. He was on a roll.

"Simple. All Oppland number plates have a two-letter prefix that begins with either 'H' or 'J'. I saw the 'JC' prefix on your number plate and thought to myself ' Yep. That's Opplund all right'.

He leant forward to try to catch the side of Jonathan's eye as best he could from the distance of the rear bench seat

"Must be like having a personalized number plate eh JC?"

Jonathan looked across at Marrielle almost accusingly.

"Your registration has JC on it? Why didn't you tell me?"

"Why should I? You could have seen it for yourself. What difference does it make?"

"It's a sign" Jonathan said turning away from Marrielle and pushing his shoulder against the door. He stared at the white lines of the slow lane as they passed by. "It's a sign. That's all" he muttered to himself.

Dugdale and Moonboots exchanged quizzical glances, not sure if they were witnessing the early onset of a domestic, and confused that the person they had assumed to be the owner of the van didn't know its registration number.

"So what do you guys do?" Dugdale asked trying to avoid any unpleasant escalation of the number plate dispute.

Marrielle glanced over at Jonathan who hunched his shoulders as if trying to disappear down a crack in the middle of his shoulder blades and pushed himself even harder against the door window.

"I'm a fiddle player. Hardanger Fiddle, if you've ever heard of it" said Marrielle.

Moonboots lifted his head and raised his eyebrows to the sky.

"Ahhh, the music of the Gods"

"... and JC, he is a silversmith. He makes beautiful things out of silver" Marrielle continued.

The two passengers made approving noises and looked suitably impressed.

"And how about you two guys?" said Marrielle "What takes you up North? Business?"

Dugdale, regarding himself as senior partner in this enterprise leaned forward "I used to be a j . . ."

"We're sort of investigators" Moonboots interrupted, giving Dugdale a sharp elbow dig as he did so "Psychic phenomena, unexplained events, folklore, that sort of thing."

Marrielle checked the mirror and saw Dugdale elbow Moonboots in the arm and then give him a look of disgust.

"Ah that's so interesting" said Marrielle, "I love that kind of thing. One time in Norway, I was driving down Trollstigen, it's like a series of hairpins? I came around one hairpin and there were a group of trolls sitting around a table eating and drinking. I swear its true. I passed by trying to get to the next hairpin to get another look, and as I turned back on myself, there was nothing there. I hadn't even been drinking. Well, not much. It was amazing."

Moonboots clicked into gear.

"You might have had a narrow escape there love. Trolls can be a bit nasty. Did you hear about the great troll hunter Eric Natterud?"

He didn't wait for an answer.

"Spent his life hunting for trolls. Police found his brand new BMW in the mountains totally wrecked, smashed to pieces. No skid marks, no other vehicle, nothing to crash into. It was ten years before the injuries finally killed him. They reckon it was the revenge of the trolls."

"Wow" said Marrielle, "I can totally believe that. So many strange things happen in those mountains. That's so cool. I mean sad, but cool. So tell me what are you investigating in Alderley Edge, are there trolls there?"

Moonboots placed his right boot on top of Dugdale's foot and pressed down hard, causing him to let out a muffled grunt.

"Ahhh . . . weeeellll . . . you'll no doubt be familiar with that classic book *The Weirdstone of Brasingamen* which was all about what goes on up on The Edge?"

"No. I've never heard of it, but you must have JC?"

Jonathan, arms tightly crossed and pulled hard into his chest, was now pressed so tightly against the window, little patches of mist were appearing where his nose touched the glass.

"Never heard of it" he muttered.

"But you must have, you live . . ." she hesitated "Didn't you live there once?"

"Yes. But I didn't get out much" he wriggled, pulled his arms tighter together, and then closed his eyes.

"So go on Moonboots what about this Weirdstone thing?"

Moonboots freewheeled as if at the bar of The Black Lion.

"Yeah, well this guy wrote the book donkey's years ago. Became a bit of a classic to people like us, you know, 'believers'.

THE ART OF BEING ONE

All about these supposedly mythical creatures that live on The Edge. He said it was fiction all along. Now people are saying, he didn't make it up, that these creatures really exist up there. We are just going to do a bit of sniffing around. See what we can find. Might be an article in it for *Alien Magazine*."

"Oh I love it. Hey you've got to let me come with you. Do you fancy that JC, a bit of pixie hunting?"

Jonathan kept his eyes tightly closed, not moving, silent.

"I think he's asleep."

Jonathan sat clutching his thighs to his chest on the grass verge, watching as Dugdale and Moonboots crouched on the floor and fiddled around in Clementine's rear engine compartment. Marrielle stood behind them trying to pop her head between the two whenever an opportunity arose, not sure of what she was looking for but wanting to offer a degree of moral support.

Eventually Dugdale pulled his head out of the engine bay. His cheek was smeared with oil and beads of sweat were rolling down his forehead.

"It's just as I thought love" he looked at Marrielle knowingly. "Had a Beetle years ago, same engine you know. She's just got a bit too hot, probably with all the extra weight."

Moonboots looked down at Dugdale's oversized girth.

Dugdale shot him a glance and carried on.

"The carb gets flooded you see. Usually, it's best to leave it for half an hour. The carb will clear and it'll give her a chance to cool down. Leave the engine flap open, get some air in there."

"Okay, great. If we are going to be sitting around for a while, JC why don't you make yourself useful and put the kettle on?"

Jonathan grunted and stepped into the van.

Moonboots walked to the side of the hedgerow, unzipped his fly and began relieving himself in full view of passing traffic. He looked up and stared across the field towards a series of large white dishes, sitting at various angles with needles pointing up to the sky.

"Jesus, Brian, that's Jodrell Bank. Keep that kettle boiling Marrielle, we're going to have a closer look."

The two followed the line of the hedgerow for a couple of hundred yards, with Moonboots keeping his eyes firmly fixed on the larger of the dishes, until they came across a small wooden stile, which opened onto a track winding roughly in the direction of Jodrell Bank.

Moonboots hopped over the stile and turned to see Dugdale stuck, with one leg on each side of the wooden construction, unsure what to do next. He grabbed his arm and levered him unceremoniously fieldside, where they both stopped and looked at each other like two schoolboys out of sight of the teacher.

"Well?" Moonboots said.

Dugdale drew breath.

"Well . . . she's a nice bird, but that JC, he's a bit of a weird one. Doesn't say much, but maybe that's how silversmiths are. I suppose they spend a lot of time on their own."

THE ART OF BEING ONE

"Brian, you're an investigative journalist now. You've been cutting and pasting match reports for too long. You've got to start seeing what's there."

Dugdale lit up a cigarette took a puff and exhaled loudly.

"What? What do mean?"

Moonboots became animated.

"I mean did you ever see a silversmith with hands like that? He's got hands the size of tennis rackets."

"And?"

"Silversmiths have to have small, nimble fingers. That's why a lot of . . ." he emphasized his words as if talking to a halfwit, ." . . *fiddle players* . . . double up as silversmiths."

There was a mocking laugh, "Yeah, and how the Hell would you know that?"

Moonboots knew he was on solid ground.

"Discovery Channel. *Hands of Silver, Strings of Gold*. I saw it a couple of months back when the pub was quiet. He's no silversmith."

Leaning back against the stile Dugdale took another drag of his cigarette.

"So what? He's probably claiming benefits and needs a cover story. And anyway Moonboots, what's with all this space detective stuff?"

Moonboots tapped his forehead and bounced his hand up into the air "You just don't see it do you Brian? Big hands, six foot two, he's not a silversmith that's for sure, its not his van evidently. They don't seem to me to be a couple. Am I making myself clear?"

"As usual, no you're not."

"He's wearing a 'tfl' jacket. Do I hear a penny dropping?"

"'tfl'?"

"Transport for flipping London, Brian. The underground?"

Dugdale's cigarette dropped to the foor.

Jonathan filled the kettle from the small sink in the back of the van fed from a plastic water container, whilst Marielle busied herself putting together a few sandwiches on a fold away table that she had set out on the grass verge.

There was an awkward silence, until Marrielle, seeing Jonathan struggling to light the burner with a match, stepped in and took over. She lit the flame and placed the kettle on top of it, giving him a look that she hoped would discourage his learned helplessness.

"Well?" she said.

"Well what?"

"You've hardly said a word since Corley Services."

He ran his hands across his stubbly beard.

"Those guys are making me nervous. I don't want to go back to my old life – not just now anyway. This pair might recognise me. Then what?"

She made him stand out on the grass verge, whilst she walked around him, surveying him up and down, front and back.

"Look at you. Your clothes are dirty. Your hair is matted and greasy. You've got a beard forming. You smell."

"I smell?"

"You smell. You are wearing a Scandinavian knit hat with

tassles. Is this how you were when you were a goalkeeper?"

He fiddled with the tassles of his hat and ran the back of his hand against the beard. He smiled.

"You know what Marrielle, you might be right."

"I am right. You look like a 'Gapper' gone wrong."

Jonathan poured some tea and tried to speak, but found it hard to get the words out, and so made a small coughing sound to try to disguise his discomfort. He made another attempt and again his mouth just seemed to lock open without any words.

"Are you trying to say something JC?"

He flushed.

"Yes. Well. I can't go home. Paparazzi, stuff like that. I was wondering. You know when we've dropped off the two . . ."

She jumped in on his hesitation "The two travelling companions?"

"Yes. When we've dropped them off, if you're not going anywhere, shall we go and sleep up on The Edge tonight?" he flushed again.

"I mean, me outside, you in the van. I didn't mean . . . .." He tailed off and looked at the floor.

She took a sip of her tea grasping it with both hands and holding it against her chin. She watched Jonathan quietly writhe in his self-conscious discomfort for a moment and smiled at the unassuming demeanor of this man who looked as if he had just returned from a shift with The British Antarctic Survey.

"Yes" she said reassuringly. "I'd like that. On The Edge with pixies, trolls and who knows what? That sounds pretty cool. You can have the guest bedroom."

"Great. There's a guest bedroom?"

"Yes. It's a tent."

In the distance there was a babble of laughter interspersed with conversation then more laughter, as Dugdale and Moonboots retraced their steps along the hedgerow back towards the van. Jonathan watched as they weaved their way along the verge, seemingly without a care in the world. The pull of an arm here, a hand on a shoulder there, an indignant look from one and then synchronised laughter from the pair as they revisited or reinvented some well-worn jocular routine. It was the stuff of camaraderie. The stuff that Jonathan had left behind. The stuff that had been taken from him when the 'incident' shattered the trust that is essential to camaraderie. The stuff that was all part of 'dying so that others may live'.

He felt a tinge of envy as he brought out two cups of tea for the pair and tried to project a more friendly face, now that he felt his own face was unrecognizable.

"Two cups of Britain's finest there lads. Any aliens out there?" he smiled.

Dugdale was panting heavily and two large circles of sweat had appeared, one under each arm.

"Nah. That thing's been there for more than half a century. All it's ever found is a load of bleedin' space rocks"

Moonboots begged to differ. "Hang on Brian. That's a serious piece of kit there. Now that it's part of the Virgin project, it's hooked into a global network of scopes. If we are looking for something and it's out there, it's going to get found."

Jonathan walked over to the hedgerow, stared at the giant white discs pointing to the sky and took a bite from a sandwich filled with cheese and chive spread from a tube.

"Yeah, well let's hope it takes a while yet. We don't want to find everything do we?"

CHAPTER SIXTEEN
PAULO HE DOTH PROTEST TOO MUCH

It was a pleasant enough evening for Dugdale and Moonboots to sit outside what once would have been a traditional village pub. Now with its monstrous prefabricated box-like extension it had joined the ranks of tired, grey, budget hotels, serving grey pallid beer and microwave food.

They each took a couple of long sips from their pints, pulling faces of mild disapproval and then they sat for a moment soaking up the gentle evening sun and grinning at each other like a pair of young lads who had just spent the evening with a woman way out of their league.

Dugdale, still grinning, shook his head from side to side.

"What are the . . . ? I mean . . . Moonboots. What are the chances of that?

Moonboots stopped grinning and put on what he considered to be his sage, wise face "It's meant to be Brian. Coincidences like that, they're not coincidences. It's the Universe telling you to do something. Imploring you to act. I'm telling you. Meeting those two was meant to be."

They tried to calculate roughly the probability of such an encounter. Considering all the small things that could have prevented them from meeting Marrielle in the Service Station shop, just at the moment that they did. If Capriolo had refused a meeting there would have been no imperative to head North; if Slates hadn't popped into the pub that lunchtime and said he had to drop off a load in Tamworth next day; if Dugdale hadn't forgotten his digital tape recorder and made Slates do a 'U' turn so he could go and get it; if that minibus hadn't caught fire on the M1, forcing all the traffic into a single lane; if Dugdale hadn't been outvoted when he wanted to stop at Watford Gap Services; if they had been dropped off at the junction after Corley instead of taking Slates' advice and trying to bum a lift at the services; if Moonboots hadn't been such a know-it-all and interrupted Marrielle whilst she was browsing a copy of *Psychologies*; if Marrielle would have taken umbrage, as so many had before, and told him to 'do one'.

It was a chance in a million, something akin to winning the lottery, but as Moonboots pointed out, someone wins every week. The chance in a million occurs all the time, it's just that we don't think about it much. If we were to analyse all the important episodes in our lives they could always have worked out differently by the interaction of dozens of seemingly small incidents and decisions. Yet Moonboots remained convinced that this meeting was no happy accident. It was some form of divine intervention. There was a reason for it. They just had to try to figure out what it was.

Dugdale replenished the drinks and threw a bag of nuts in the general direction of Moonboots. "Now what?"

Moonboots ripped open the bag and laid the nuts across the middle of the table. "We need to think about strategy. Strategy and tactics."

There was a cough and a splutter as Dugdale tried to swallow a mouthful of nuts whilst simultaneously failing to suppress his laughter. He took a swig of ale to try to swill down the nuts and chuckled again.

"Moonboots, you've been unemployed for twenty years. What would you know about strategy?"

It was an open invitation. An opportunity for Moonboots to explain the art and science of remaining successfully unemployed for twenty years. For him it was a lifestyle choice, which had meant staying ahead of the game. With over 117 unemployment benefit rule changes during his 'career', the only way to continually thrive and survive was to stay ahead of the game. He had systematically researched Green Papers, White Papers and Policy Directives to the extent that by the time they came into force he often knew more about the rules than the benefits staff that he had to deal with. That was his strategy element, see the big picture and think a few moves ahead. He believed that strategy alone was not enough, and he liked to think of tactics as part of a series of ongoing mini-battles, 'small movements in front of enemy lines' as he liked to call them. He would antagonize, create grey areas and occasionally surprise and charm the benefits staff, to the point where he had, albeit begrudgingly, legendary status amongst them.

Dugdale took a long sip of his beer and looked at Moonboots with mild admiration. "You mean all these years you've been standing in the pub, and we've felt sorry for you and kept you in beer . . ." his face turned to disgust ." . . and it was a lifestyle choice?"

"We're all free to make our own choices Brian. The system is there, I don't make the rules. I made my choice and I make the rules work to my advantage. Politicians do the same, except they get to make the rules as well. So which shall we talk about first, strategy or tactics?"

"Erm, well I guess we should . . . what do you think Moonboots?"

He'd already thought through various scenarios in his head. Strategically he felt that they were in a very powerful position, as long as they could win and maintain the trust of both sides of the equation, Capriolo and Jonathan, for as long as possible until they determined their 'out', or, as Moonboots now liked to call it, 'the optimal monetization scenario'.

Marrielle might be a key influencer. They would have to handle her with care, and if Dugdale could become a trusted confidante of Jonathan, they could get an exclusive on the full inside story of the disappearing goalkeeper, plus, if they played their cards right, some valuable image rights. They could even cut Jonathan in if necessary.

THE ART OF BEING ONE

If Jonathan got spooked or wouldn't play ball, then there was the option to sell information leading to his whereabouts to his employers, on the grounds that he felt sure that the club would want to end a damaging PR episode and reclaim a valuable asset. That was the strategy and they would have to choose the defining moment.

First they had to begin to 'make small movements in front of enemy lines'.

The moment the door of Café Vincenzo opened, it's patron ran around to the front of his refrigerated counter and stood in front of Dugdale and Moonboots. His shoulders were pushed back and he had an indignant look on his face as though they had insulted him just by walking through the door.

"We is full" Vincenzo said with total certainty.

The pair looked at each other, stared at the seven empty tables, then looked at each other again. Vincenzo pursed his lips and nodded once before folding his arms. He was in no mood to move out of their way.

"How do you define full?" asked Dugdale with a smile trying to make a joke of the situation.

Vincenzo bunched his fingers together and thrust them in front of his face.

"I no have to define full. I am the boss here, if I say we are full, we are full. Is simple."

With that he turned and walked towards the back of his domain, and with a dramatic flourish pulled out seven small cards covered with plastic laminate. At each table he flipped a card like a gambler delivering a winning hand and said "Reserved." When he reached the seventh table, he paused for a moment and looked at his would be customers as if he might be about to reconsider his position, before banging the last card on the table and drawing out the word.

"Re-seeeer-ved."

"But there's nobody here" said Moonboots.

"Can't you read? Every table it say 'reserved'. That mean we is full. Now you go"

Dugdale was beginning to get annoyed "You're taking the ..."

"Brian" a voice said from behind. It was Capriolo still with his scarf pulled around his neck despite the warm spring sunshine.

"Vincenzo, these men are with me. We have a meeting"

Vincenzo stood his ground for a moment and eyed the pair suspiciously from top to toe, before walking to the back of the café and picking up one of his laminated signs, wiping it down with his apron, and sliding it into his pocket.

"You are lucky. We have a cancellation." He walked back behind his refrigerated counter and into his small back room kitchen. There was the sound of a metal tray hitting the ground hard followed by barrage of cursing in Italian. At one point Capriolo winced at one of his outbursts and quietly said "Whoa Vincenzo."

"I don't think we ask for coffee just yet" said Capriolo "We let him calm down."

THE ART OF BEING ONE

Dugdale and Capriolo reminisced about the times that they had crossed swords at various press conferences over the years. Capriolo gave him a stern lecture on the stupidity of some of his questioning and how insensitive and disrespectful it could sometimes be.

Dugdale tried to interject once or twice, but felt the gentle tap of a Moonboot on his ankle each time he tried to do so. Eventually, Capriolo finished, uninterrupted, sat back in his chair and gave a long sigh. It was as if a great burden had been lifted off his shoulders.

It was a chance for Dugdale to profer a polite defence of the journalist's lot and the need to fill column inches, especially when nothing spectacular had happened out on the pitch. Capriolo grunted a few times but waited until Dugdale had finished his pitch before he spoke. He sat silent for a moment, then pursed his lips and offered his hand to Dugdale.

"Is business Brian, that is all. Is not personal. We all have our job to do. Okay we work together now eh?"

Moonboots felt it was time to get down to business. "Shall we talk about the Christie situation Mr Capriolo. We feel that we have some information that may be valuable to you."

Capriolo looked like he was pondering this for a moment. "Yes, we talk business in a moment. First, Brian I want your advice on something."

Dugdale raised his eyebrows. Roberto Capriolo wanted his advice? After three years of treating him like 'The Invisible Man'?

Reaching into his inside jacket pocket, Capriolo pulled out an A4 piece of paper that had been folded in four, opened it out and spread it on the table.

"I like your country" he said waving his arm in the direction of the street outside. "I take my bike into the hills. I have your cups of tea. I even went fishing for trout. Now I think it is time to understand something of the culture, yes?"

Dugdale and Moonboots looked at each other and nodded approvingly.

"But tell me Brian. You are a man of words. Tell me. I try to understand your Shakespeare, but I struggle. For example, this I print from the internet, what does this mean?"

He passed the A4 sheet over to Dugdale. Moonboots pulled his chair slightly behind him so he could read over his shoulder.

Before Dugdale, had finished, Moonboots stepped in.

"Ah Hamlet. That's the famous scene where the Queen says 'The lady doth protest too much'."

"Si. But I no understand. What does this mean?"

Dugdale tried to interject, but Moonboots had already begun a monologue which explained how the meaning of the word 'protest' had changed over the centuries and that the line delivered by the Queen in Hamlet had taken on a more subtle meaning than its original literal one.

Capriolo listened with interest. "I'm still confused" he said.

Dugdale stepped in. "Roberto, usually when we say in English that someone protests too much, we tend to mean that they have something to hide, so they make a big protest in order to cover it up."

The Italian sat trying to take this in. He moved his head to one side and gave a single nod, then did the same on the other side, before furrowing his brow.

"So let me get this straight. Suppose a manager knows his

player has made a dive to get the penalty. He protest about the referee, he protest about the pitch, he protest about the fans, the weather, the TV pundits, everything. He protest, he protest, he protest. Hmmm. He protest too much. He do this because he have something to hide."

Dugdale smiled broadly proud of his new student.

"That's exactly right Roberto. Spot on."

For a moment Capriolo's eyes flashed with delight that he had understood the subtlety of the point, and then his face saddened and his shoulders slumped slightly. Quietly, almost imperceptibly he whispered Paulo's name as if he had just thrown a handful of earth onto his coffin.

CHAPTER SEVENTEEN
TREE HUGGER

Marrielle awoke like a child at Christmas and jumped out of the van into the National Trust car park, still wearing her pyjamas.

Smiling broadly she surveyed the landscape. Dark, natural, untamed woodland interspersed with the occasional open fields and random outcrops of beautiful bronze rock leading to a five-hundred foot sandstone escarpment known as 'The Edge', which plummeted to the lush green flatlands below.

She couldn't suppress her laughter on seeing the wooden signpost by the side of the tent where Jonathan lay still sleeping. "To the Edge" it said pointing towards a rough track with randomly placed cobblestones.

She jiggled the tent pole. There was a short grunt from inside.

"Listen to this" she said reading place names from a leaflet she had picked up from the bulletin board at the edge of the car park.

"Stormy Point; The Wizard's Well; The Hermit; Goldenstone; The Holy Well; Saddlebole . . ." She feigned a spooky voice ." . . this sounds to me like the kind of place where pixies do dwell."

The zipper of the tent buzzed. A bearded Jonathan still wearing the knitted hat with pigtails squeezed his head through the tent flap and rubbed his eyes.

"Look" said Marrielle "I found a map. Let's go pixie hunting."

"Let me see the map."

He lay on his back and held the small leaflet between his eyes and the sky. Smiling gently he whispered the names slowly like someone who had difficulty reading.

"Gol-den-stone; Wiz-ar-ds We-ll" and for a moment he was lost in time.

Marrielle slipped back into the van and searched for some suitable pixie hunting attire.

"Slow down JC"

Marrielle called after Jonathan as he strode along a track clutching what had now become 'his map', stopping only occasionally to check his bearings or align himself with some distant landmark. He paused and allowed Marrielle to catch up.

"Relax" she said, "We have all day. What's your hurry?"

THE ART OF BEING ONE

He looked out towards a large sycamore tree that had taken a tumble during the winter, its branches taken off by a chainsaw, revealing beautiful concentric patterns at intervals along the flattened trunk. Then he rubbed his hand along a sandstone boulder, slightly moist with morning dew, and took a deep breath.

"It's just this." He said incredulously, holding his arms out wide. "All of this. I never ever did this before. Used a map for real. I've lived in this area for years and never ever been to this place. What have I been doing?"

Marrielle frowned "Yes. What have you been doing?"

"Don't know. I obviously should have got out more."

She leaned into him as he pointed out approximately where he thought they were and prized his hand away from one side of the map so that they could hold it between them. There was a momentary power struggle as Jonathan gently tried to regain control. Firmly, she moved his other hand away and took hold of the map, ignoring his protests.

"Let me have a go at deciding which way we go" she said playfully.

"I liked the sound of that place 'Wizard's Well'. It sounds so spooky. Shall we go to Wizard's Well?"

She could see that he was uncomfortable without 'his map' and agreed to return it provided he figured out a route that would take them there. He traced out a route with his finger, via Engine Vein and The Beacon, pointing out to Marrielle the circuitous curve of the track, even though Wizards Well was quite close by as the crow flies.

"Okay," she said, "Let's go off piste, and go straight there."

He couldn't reconcile this thought. For one it involved rule breaking. The pathways and tracks were made for people to follow. Secondly, it was Marrielle that said there was no hurry. He was confused.

She smiled enthusiastically. "Come on. It'll be fun. Let's just go this way. Who knows what we might find. Pixies, trolls, wizards. Let's do it."

He regarded his map once again, uncomfortably checking the broad direction that they should take to get to Wizard's Well directly. He hesitated and looked unsure of himself.

Marrielle stepped off the track and into a wooded area. He didn't move. She stepped back again and held out her hand encouragingly.

"Come on JC. Put your map away for a minute. It's all about serendipity, remember?"

Reluctantly, he carefully folded up his map, unzipped his Velcro pocket and placed it carefully alongside his Travelcard. He took hold of Marielle's hand and they picked their way through an area of wild woodland with saplings leaning this way and that and thickets of rich green fern sprouting from a soft spongy carpet of decaying leaves and humous.

In just a few minutes, barely a hundred metres from the rambling path, it felt like another world. It was dark with occasional rays of sunlight piercing through the canopy like shards of crystal. At Marrielle's prompting they stood under the spotlight of the sunbeams and held their faces up to the sky. She raised her arms above her head in a long stretch and feeling the warmth on her face let out a long, satisfied "Mmmmmmmm" noise. "Can you feel that JC? Can you feel the life force running through you?"

He coughed nervously. "I can feel the sun and that's nice."

He fidgeted wondering what to do with his arms, so he folded them firmly across his chest.

She brought her hands down slowly in an elaborate arc, before drawing them together in front of her heart as if she were in prayer. She inhaled deeply then exhaled loudly, then brought her hands to her sides and gently smiled to herself.

"Oh JC, you are closed to it. You must soak it all up. Look at you with your arms crossed. How will you ever embrace nature's magic like that?"

"But it's just a bit of sunbathing. It's just in the woods that's all."

She moved closer to him and spoke quietly almost in a whisper as though she had a secret to share.

"No. It's more than that. This is a magical place, I can feel it. I know about these things. There's something here for us. We must absorb the earth energy. If we allow it to, it will seep into us through osmosis."

He wasn't quite sure what osmosis was, but he let it pass. Only a week ago if someone had talked of magic, earth energy and nature they would have been laughed out of the dressing room. Yet now in the light and shade of the woodland; in the quietness punctuated by birdsong; in amongst the cracking of twigs and rustling of leaves; anything seemed possible.

"Sooo . . . how do we do that then?" he asked looking at her breasts as if they had suddenly and miraculously only just appeared.

She clasped her hands together excitedly "First we will start by hugging a tree and then we will do some meditation."

He jolted his head backwards. "Whoa. Hug a tree? Hold on, I've heard about those tree huggers."

"Yes, and what have you heard?"

He had to think for a moment.

"Well that they . . . well . . . that they hug trees and things like that."

"Things like what?"

He knew he was unable to elaborate. Truth be told, he knew precious little about tree huggers, just that whatever it was that they did was frowned upon in the dressing room culture.

"Tree hugging." He said, "They do that tree hugging stuff."

"Yes, and did you ever hear of anyone coming to any harm as a result of tree hugging?"

He had to admit that he hadn't. He knew that he had never knowingly met a tree hugger. Come to think of it he hadn't seen or read anything about the subject for a long, long time, or maybe he never had. It was just 'out there' that tree huggers were one thing and footballers were something altogether different.

Marrielle wandered around rubbing her palms along the bark of several of the more substantial trees, with the air of someone who was listening for something. Eventually, she had decided.

"Okay JC, you take the big oak and I'll take the sycamore."

He looked at her helplessly as if she had just addressed him in Swahili.

"Which is the oak?" he asked sheepishly.

She directed him and they each took their positions by their respective trees. He opted for the vertical tree hug and followed Marrielle's instructions to first feel the bark with his palms before spending some time smelling it. When prompted he stared up along the trunk to the top of the tree, saw the powerful branches reaching out in the goalkeepers 'ready' position and tried to imagine the vastness of the deep root system. He was ready. He placed his cheek against the bark and even with his giant span he only managed to embrace one third of the trunk. He felt small and insignificant. This was unchartered territory for a goalkeeper who had spent a lifetime perfecting the art of looking big and being significant.

Marrielle embraced her sycamore lovingly, and with her cheek almost caressing the smooth bark, called calmly across to Jonathan.

"Now just relax and try to absorb the energy of the tree. Give out love and it will give you love back. Close your eyes and just be. Let the tree energy take you wherever it takes you."

His body was taut at first. He noticed that there was nothing. Nothing but silence, him and the oak. This mighty thing that had stood solid for hundreds of years. He relaxed and felt strangely soothed by the presence and attention of this thing that made him feel so small. He tried to soak up the energy as Marrielle had suggested and wondered if he was doing it right. Then he tried to give out love. He struggled. This was even harder than absorbing the tree energy.

He wondered if he had ever known love. Was that a kind of love that his mum had given to him before the cancer had taken her away? A love that knew no hugs. Was that a kind of love that he'd known with his odd encounters with odd girlfriends? A love that knew no depth. Was that a kind of love, his total dedication to his job, to the point where he had sacrificed himself for the team? A love destroyed by Fanni and Mushi.

He tried once again to find the source of his love. He waited for it to burst out from some wellspring deep inside him, but nothing happened. He wondered if he actually possessed any love at all. Perhaps he had over compensated for his lack of love by giving everything he had, almost every waking moment, every sinew, every breathe to the team; the job; the manager.

It was as if an electric current had been tripped when the tree seemed to yield its grip over Jonathan. He fell backwards to the floor landing in a bed of bracken and lay for a moment, dazed, looking up at the twigs and branches of the canopy through which small puffy white clouds made their way across the blue sky.

Marrielle stood over him, hands on hips, looking on with a mixture of amusement and concern.

"You found that interesting?" she said.

He rubbed the side of his face where his cheek had been pressed up against the bark and a small smear of blood spread across his fingers.

"Shit. Something happened there. Don't ask me what it was but something happened. It was like a force."

She held out a hand to help him up and dusted him down to remove bits of leaf and bark from his clothes.

"So now you are a tree hugger JC. I have to say I never ever before saw a tree hugger land on their back. You must be a special one"

He smiled confidently at Marrielle, stood straight and then stared at the oak tree.

"Maybe I am Marrielle. Maybe I'm *the* special one."

CHAPTER EIGHTEEN

TROLL HUNTERS

One hundred and eight steps had been dug into the rugged woodland hillside, each now a hardened bank of earth, held in by a wooden stave, and leading in a higgledy-piggledy fashion from the flatlands below to a rough track not far from Holy Well high up on The Edge.

It was not unusual to see a couple of well kitted out ramblers stopping two thirds of the way up to catch their breath. Dugdale and Moonboots though looked somehow incongruous. Two overweight middle-aged men, stopping as early as the twenty-fifth step, dripping with sweat and each ripping a can from their respective six packs. They burst open the ring-pull at precisely the same moment and took large glugs of ale in between gulping for air.

"We should have taken a taxi" Dugdale said, running his

shirt sleeve across his brow and mopping up some substantial globules of sweat.

Moonboots parked himself a few steps higher up and surveyed the landscape.

"Better we do it this way Brian. We need to get the lay of the land if we're going to seem convincing to Marrielle. Besides you need to shift some of that timber you're carrying."

Dugdale was about to object and then looked down at his protruding gut. He prepared himself to retaliate, and then pulled back in resignation.

"Yes. You're right. I need to sort myself out. But that can come later, we're on the verge of something big here let's not blow it. You keep Marrielle occupied and I'll try and win the trust of Christie."

"JC remember? You've got to remember to call him JC, otherwise he'll know we are onto him, then we will have blown it."

Dugdale repeated 'JC' over and over until he felt sure that it was locked into his brain. There was a newly emerging respect for Moonboots. He had always enjoyed his company, within reason, but got irritated by his know-it-all tendencies and some of his bizarre claims, yet seeing him operate in a real situation, away from the bar in The Black Lion, was proving to be a revelation. He had an uncanny ability to absorb information, almost just by standing there, which he must have honed at the bar over the years. Earlier they had spent a full two hours in the library, with Moonboots reviewing every tourist leaflet and map he could lay his hands on, even managing to flirt with the librarian in the 'Local History' section. When an elderly Mancunian couple began ferreting around for information, he waited for his moment, stepped into their conversation and was soon into full flow about the six gold bars that were found on The Edge in 1993, 1997 and one that was found in the sixties, but as he pointed out, had only been handed in to the authorities after the later finds were declared treasure trove.

Dugdale's first reaction was to grimace as he normally did when Moonboots cornered another couple of 'victims' for one of his monologues. But having had access to all of the same information and only absorbed a fraction of it, he had to admit to having a sneaking admiration for someone, who could remember all of that, and deliver it as though he had been a tourist guide all of his life.

Moonboots continued in this vein as they passed the wizard's head that had been carved into the rock close by Wizard's Well, a natural spring, he pointed out, dating back to pagan times. He stood trying to make out the inscription below the head that was partially obscured by moss.

'Drink of this and take thy fill for the water falls by the Wizhard's Will'

Dugdale couldn't resist pointing out what he referred to as a 'typo' in 'Wizhards', but the look of contempt given to him by Moonboots was enough to dampen any thoughts he may have had of a comedy riff.

Moonboots knelt by the well as if he was about to pray, and then cupped his hands together to scoop a trickle of water into his mouth.

"Try it Brian, they say that the water from this well increases your fertility."

"That's the last thing I need. I'll have one of these thanks"

Dugdale said tearing a can from his six pack and tossing on in the direction of Moonboots.

Instead of throwing the empty cans into the undergrowth, as they had done before, Moonboots, carefully rinsed both of them, and knelt down to fill them with water from Wizards Well. He handed one can to Dugdale and held onto one himself.

"These are for Marrielle and the lad. She'll like that. You wait and see."

When the pair arrived, Marrielle was sitting alone in a trestle chair, quietly watching the occasional car or van drift by eagerly awaiting their 'pixie hunting' trip as she liked to call it.

Moonboots enthusiastically proffered the two cans of Wizard's Well spring water, along with an elaborate explanation of its origins. She held the cans each with just two fingers and at some distance away from her, as if holding a petri dish containing some unusual form of fungal growth.

Moonboots tried to reassure her.

"There's one for you and one for JC. They say it increases your fertility." He checked himself "Er, sorry, I didn't mean to . . . I'm not even sure if you're a couple. I don't mean to pry."

"You are not, and we are not" she said walking across to the hedgerow set back from the lay-by.

"Thank you for the gift, but I can't drink this. It's contaminated with traces of stale beer and . . ." she looked at the areas around the ring pulls ." . . and who knows what else?"

She poured the contents around the base of a rhododendron bush "There, now we shall have beautiful fertile flowers."

Dugdale raised an eyebrow in the direction of Moonboots

as if he had just a recovered a point in some game of strategy, and then tried to be inconspicuous as he peered inside the van.

"Where is he then. JC, where's he gone?" He said, hiding his concern well.

They watched Marrielle fold up her chair and load it into the rear of the van. "Oh, JC you know, he's a funny guy, a bit unusual."

They followed her as she fiddled with the sliding door at the side of the van trying several times to close it, before a final heave slammed it tight into its lock.

"So where did he go? Did he say where he was going?" Dugdale asked.

"Yes he did" she smiled "Now stick your beers underneath Clementine and let's go pixie hunting. Where shall we start Mr Moonboots?"

Dugdale's shoulders slumped as he felt a moonboot stand on his toe "Calm down. You're too eager" Moonboots muttered "Just leave it to me."

Moonboots proffered his arm to Marrielle. "If you ask me Marrielle, I think the area bounded by The Druids Circle, Wizard's Well and Holy Well would be a good place to start to look for any evidence of 'non-humanoid' settlements."

She took his arm excitedly "Cool show me the way Mr Moonboots."

CHAPTER NINETEEN
THE HERMIT

The area known locally as 'The Hermit' had once been the home to John Evans a recluse who had built a log cabin, now long disappeared, next to a cave that he used as a larder and for storing chemicals and equipment that he used for analyzing rocks.

Now all that remained was a drainage ditch, a few flagstones that had formed the base for the cabin and the outline of the garden that Evans had created along with a rough stone terrace.

Jonathan sat on one of Marrielle's embroidered quilts and looked out from the cave. In the early evening sunshine it felt warm and secure and with the trees embracing the whole area, it gave him the feeling of being inside a small cocoon.

He had prepared himself a small sleeping area on a flat part of the cave floor, which he had lined with ferns to make a green springy mattress. On top of that was the pillow and quilt that Marrielle had brought from the van. A flat, shelf-like piece of rock supported a battery operated lantern, one of Marrielle's favourite cups and a bottle of drinking water.

"Now what?" he said, and looked around the cave as if expecting an answer.

He crawled out to the edge of the cave then wandered around the remnants of what had been a home to 'The Hermit', wondering if he might be able to bring the garden back to life. Perhaps even grow his own food. If a Hermit had made his life here, why couldn't he?

In his mind he began compiling a list of jobs that would have to be done to make this place habitable. He picked up loose rocks and began arranging them close to the mouth of the cave, constructing a circular hearth capable of hosting the fire that he imagined would be at the heart of his new home.

It had been a long time since he had sat in front of a real fire.

He could remember it clearly, his cheeks burning at the thought of himself sitting in Principal Readfearn's office the day he was called in with his clothing muddy and torn and his fists grazed and bloody.

"I'm disappointed in you Christie. You're supposed to be one of the good guys" Redfearn had said raking the coals of his open fire and throwing on another log.

"Davies has been taken to hospital. It looks like it will become a police matter. You could be in serious trouble. You could go down for this."

All he was trying to do was to eke out some justice after Davies had abused a smaller, younger boy.

THE ART OF BEING ONE

"What was I supposed to do?" Jonathan had protested, "Let the bastard get away with it?"

Redfearn pulled his chair closer "You know what we say here Christie. When you are faced with injustice, behave yourself with as much dignity as you can for as long as you can. In time the truth will be seen."

The truth of what Redfearn did to Jonathan that day in return for not calling the police was never seen. Years later, after Jonathan had responded to a request from the Children's Home for a batch of tickets for a match, Redfearn had appeared in the players' lounge surrounded by 'his boys' tipping a knowing wink to Jonathan as he signed autographs for the kids.

He hated himself for not speaking out, yet he felt that there was some honour in the silence he had held, waiting for the truth to make its appearance. He was still waiting, and now he had been asked to maintain another silence, to brush away another injustice. Die so that others may live.

Redfearn had taken care of the police and in time Jonathan became immune to the abuse. He conditioned himself to see it as just another physical routine, just like diving at the feet of an oncoming forward. If you did it often enough it was possible not to feel anything. He still thought about what he had done to Davies though.

That made him feel sick. A moment of madness that on reflection had frightened him as he had lost control and some weird form of animal instinct had kicked in and taken over his body.

Jonathan scratched the earth with a flattened branch to make a flat bed for the fire, then stopped and stared up towards the tree canopy. He spoke aloud, giving himself a reassuring pep talk.

"Redfearn, Fanni and Mushi, they're all carved from the same wood. The truth will be seen mate. It's only a matter of time."

The tree canopy took on the form of a water colour painting as his tears began to flow.

"Just behave yourself with as much dignity as you can for as long as you can."

Wandering amongst the ferns that had weaved pathways between the randomly spaced trees, Jonathan noticed how the saplings had established themselves wherever shafts of light could penetrate the canopy. Their survival, he thought, a combination of chance and environmental conditions that could be jeopardised by a single act, malicious or accidental. As if to illustrate the point, he angled his foot against a small spindly oak sapling that had sprung from an acorn tossed from its nearby parent, then pushed sharply against it. The spindle bent as if holding off a force ten gale, then after a stamp, splintered near its base to reveal a soft white flesh, the woodland equivalent of a baby's bottom.

He bent and rubbed his fingers against the moist white splinters and chastised himself for such a vicious act. Unprovoked, unnecessary, thoughtless, as if the animal instinct that had hopsitalised Davies was still inside him, trying to get out. He tried to right the sapling but the splintered sinews were not strong enough to hold it upright, and it glided to the floor as if reaching to make a fingertip save from a thirty-yard volley.

A large oak, the mother tree, seemed to rise up over him. Standing tall like a mother about to eke out revenge to a young man who had hurt her offspring, he imagined her with her arms crossed and with a face burning with rage. Panic began to set in as he again tried to right the sapling, his eyes constantly flitting between sapling and parent as if expecting a giant hand to swoop down and slap the side of his head so hard that his ear would turn crimson and burn. He held the splintered base tightly in his fist and closed his eyes, willing the damage he had caused to heal, then made three pulsing actions and with each one whispered one, two, three. Gently he released his grip and for a split second the sapling stood tall again before wilting to the forest floor.

The mother oak seemed to him have grown taller, closer, darker and more threatening, causing him to jump up and hold out his palms in a conciliatory gesture. "Wait. I'll be back" talking to the tree as if it were a normal thing to do.

He jogged his way through rough terrain, scouring the forest floor for something that he could use as a kind of tourniquet to support the young saplings broken core until it could heal over the wound that he had inflicted. Running in circles and then zig-zags, he began picking up pieces of bark, pulling up handfuls of ferns and hoping that some walker had dropped an item of clothing that could be put to use as a makeshift bandage. Moving further away from the mother tree in desperate search of suitable materials he entered a small clearing where dappled sunlight flitted about over the base of a diseased horse chestnut that had been recently felled. It had the look of an elegant dining table. A crystal glass stood next to an open bottle of Chianti and an oval platter containing Parma ham, slices of pecorino cheese and a length of ciabatta. Jonathan walked across to the tree stump and surveyed the scene for a moment, putting down his bundle of scraps of bark and ferns. There was a book lying open next to the platter of food *On the Map – Why the world looks the way it does*, which he lifted and began to read the synopsis.

"What are you doing?" said a voice a few feet away on the edge of the clearing.

Startled, Jonathan turned quickly. "Paulo?" he said without thinking, caught unawares, the name jerked from his mouth in a reflex reaction.

Paulo moved forward cautiously trying to size up the interloper and assess whether he would be a danger. He was dirty, tall and wiry with a slightly wild look. A drug addict perhaps, a vagrant trying to steal his food.

"So, you recognise my face, but why you mess with my stuff?" He said trying to project an air of menace.

"I didn't know it was your stuff, I was just passing. I just liked the look of the book."

Quizically, Paulo looked Jonathan up and down and came closer, walking around the other side of the tree stump eyeing him up, both back and front.

"Jonathan?" He said quietly "You are Jonathan Christie . . . what the . . . ?"

"Paulo please, don't betray me. I can't. I just can't go back. Not yet anyway. Don't say that you saw me. Please."

"Betray you? You who betrayed your team, your family. I should come over there and spit in your face" he said with venom and instead spat on the ground. He knew Jonathan's physical capabilities better than most, and with his height advantage, and the absence of any other teammates to break up a fight, he had instinctively calculated that a dramatic spitting gesture was much safer than the real thing which could provoke a ruckus that he could not win.

"You would have no team if I hadn't kept quiet about what your two Uruguayan mates tried to do to me. I can still destroy your team, the project, if I choose to. Right now I am choosing to 'die so that others may live' like Capriolo asked. You call that betrayal?"

Paulo leaned forward like a boxer going in for a quick jab and snatched the book from Jonathan's hand "Give me my book you traitor" then closed it and smoothed his hands across the front and back covers before carefully examining the spine for any damage.

"Traitor? You are just like Capriolo, you would sell your own mother just to get what you want."

This time Paulo ignored the physical odds and slapped Jonathan hard across his left cheek.

Jonathan knew exactly what the unwritten rules of dressing room culture required him to do at this moment. He felt the horrible surge of adrenaline running up from his abdomen into his arms and up into the back of his head. He stood for a moment rocking slightly backwards and forwards trying to get a grip of the intense urge to smash Paulo into a pulp the way that he had done when he had hospitalised young Davies. His fists clenched and tightened and stopping them from whirling in the direction of Paulo felt like holding back a pair of dumbbells at the end of a free weights session. He breathed deeply three times, and then turned his head to look to the left, proffering his right cheek in the direction of Paulo.

"Go on Paulo. You can smack this one for Capriolo. Go ahead. And whilst you're here, chop off my bollocks and give one each to those two queers that you call family."

Paulo stood still.

"Come on Paulo. What are you waiting for?"

Gently placing the book on the tree stump table, Paulo again ran a hand across the cover as if in a gentle caress.

"Jonathan. I no want to hit you. I always like you" he said as his eyes welled with tears "You are like me. We are not like the others."

CHAPTER TWENTY

THE ANT & DEC OF TROLL HUNTERS

Marrielle skipped along in front of Dugdale and Moonboots as they made their way back to the van to pick up what was left of their six packs.

"I'm telling you I saw something Brian" she said, extending her arms to emphasise her belief in what she was saying. "Something definitely ran out of that stone circle. I saw it with my own eyes."

Dugdale refused to get carried away, despite Moonboots nudging him with his elbow.

"You're just as bad as Moonboots Marrielle. If you want to see something badly enough you will. You're imagining things."

She turned and stopped in her tracks, placing her hands on her hips.

"You don't believe me. I thought you were an investigator of the unexplained?"

He opened his mouth, but nothing came out. He stood looking uncomfortable until Moonboots stepped in.

"Yes, but we're a team you see. You need a believer and a sceptic, otherwise you can get carried away. We're a double act like Ant & Dec, Starsky & Hutch, The Two Ronnies. You know how it works."

The names meant nothing to Marrielle, but she grasped the point.

"You mean like good cop, bad cop?"

Dugdale recovered his composure "Yes. That's exactly it. That's us. Fighting for justice for the little people. But it has to be legit you see, you can't just imagine it or make it up, you have to have evidence, just like the police."

"So what are you saying? I'm an unreliable witness?"

"Not at all Marrielle. It's just that we need corroboration that's all. We can have another sortie tomorrow if you want. Now what about the lad? He'll be lonely in that cave. Shouldn't we be dropping him off some supplies?"

"JC? He'll be okay for a while. I think he needs a bit of space more than anything at the moment."

Back at the van Moonboots lay on the floor and stretched his arm under the chassis to slide out their beer stash. He handed one of his cans to Marrielle. She prepared to open it only for him to place his hand on top of hers.

"Hold on Marrielle. We have this quaint English tradition. After three. Ready. One, two . . ."

Dugdale interjected "Stop. No this doesn't seem right to me. The lad's in there." he nodded over to the forest "Spending his first night in his new home. On his own. We ought to go and have a little house warming party surely?"

Marrielle grimaced and looked down at her unopened can. She thought for a moment and then slid open the side door of Clementine.

"Okay. We should go and see if he's all right. I'll get a few things together for him."

She pulled out a folded canvas bag and began to fill it with miscellaneous items. A toilet roll; a box of Swan Vesta matches; a pamphlet on The Wonders of the Edge; half a box of Dairylea cheese triangles; a quarter bottle of Aquavit; some Ryvita crispbreads which she removed from the packet and placed in an airtight plastic container.

"This should keep him going for a while. Now let's see if we can find our way to his place. I think it was down here" she said, closing the van door and heading along a track and into the forest canopy.

It was not easy for Marrielle to retrace her steps back to The Hermit, where she had left Jonathan earlier in the day. Each track seemed just like another and Dugdale was becoming anxious.

"Are you sure you know where you are going Marrielle. I'm sure we passed that rock ten minutes ago."

"Be patient" she said stopping and surveying the landscape to get her bearings. It was near here somewhere. It's difficult because I was coming the other way."

A narrow stone drainage channel protruded from the undergrowth to act as Marrielle's anchor point. They followed it through a thicket and into the clearing that was The Hermit. Marrielle placed her finger over her lips and gently shushed the other two. She whispered, "Look he's made himself a little fireplace" then tilted her head to one side and looked at it "How sweet."

They crept towards the cave entrance where they could see the glow of a battery operated lantern and organized themselves so that Marrielle could orchestrate the surprise.

She popped her head around the entrance "Cuckooooo" she said in a high-pitched tone. "We've come to give you a . . .." She stepped through the threshold and halted abruptly.

Paulo sat by the lantern with a quilt wrapped around him reading his book and holding a half empty wine glass that took on an exaggerated crystalline look against the harsh backdrop of the cave, almost as if it were diamond encrusted.

"What you do?" he said startled and slightly embarrassed by his stone age chic appearance.

Marrielle stretched out her hands as if holding Dugdale and Moonboots at bay like a couple of reluctant guard dogs, whilst they all took a moment to register what they were seeing.

"We're looking for JC. He's our friend. He erm . . . kind of lives here we think."

"JC? You mean Jonathan? He never mention anyone to me." Paulo eyed them suspiciously as though he had caught them trying to trespass on his own property. "I don't like. You have a smell about you. The smell of . . ." his eyes looked up and locked onto Dugdale "The smell of the journalist."

Moonboots and Marrielle both looked at Dugdale who lifted his arm to his nose and sniffed.

Paulo rested his wine glass on the stone ledge by the lamp and stood up to face Dugdale, still with the quilt wrapped around him.

"I pride myself on the fact that I never forget a face. With you is easy, you also come with the rancid smell of that shitty paper you work for."

Dugdale protested "Used to work for. I don't do that anymore, I'm independent now. Professional like." He held out his hand "Brian. Brian Dugdale."

"Pffff" Paulo turned sideways and looked at Dugdale's hand in disgust "I no shake the hand of a man who deals in lies and betrayal."

Marrielle tried to break the tension.

"What's going on? Do you two know each other?"

Dugdale brushed Marrielle aside. "Brian Dugdale never lies" he said defiantly, whilst Moonboots looked askance at the idea of him referring to himself in the third person.

"Paulo, your gaffer speaks in code. My job was to interpret the code as best I could. If he called a spade a spade there would be no misunderstandings."

"Spade, code, what you talk about? You suggest that Roberto Capriolo does not tell the truth?"

"No" Dugdale held out his palms "I'm not saying that Paulo. It's just that he sometimes sees only what he wants to see. He leaves a lot of blank spaces. You can't print blank spaces. I just had to fill them in as best I could."

Deep in the forest, Jonathan removed his yellow jacket and laid it flat on the floor. He brought up the two arms and tied them together in a large double knot in order to make a kind of carrying handle for his improvised wood carrier.

Foraging around he began collecting old, dry branches, discarding those with traces of moss or those that had been exposed to recent rain. He set out three piles next to his jacket. Dry twigs suitable for kindling, modest branches for accelerating the fire and a small pile of substantial branches and trunk offcuts left by the woodsmen that would prolong the burn. He would need to come back to collect these. They were too big to fit into his jacket.

After a while he stood and folded his arms, proudly looking at his three piles, admiring the order as if it were a fascinating piece of modern art. A smile spread across his face, and he kneeled and tidied each pile a bit more. He ran his hands along the bark of some of the bigger pieces until he felt the rub of something that was not bark. A hessian patch, now grey, pitted with sap and lichen and almost indistinguishable from the bark, had at some stage been stuck on to prevent disease entering a vulnerable area. Jonathan picked at it for a moment, trying to loosen a corner, gently as if removing his own sticking plaster.

"Shit" he said, "That little tree I broke and its mum. I said I'd be back."

THE ART OF BEING ONE

He pulled at the hessian flap, taking the sharp end of a smaller branch and trying to lever an opening. It was stuck fast, but he continued until he was able to prize open a flap big enough to accommodate three fingers. Even in the world of hessian flaps, the 80:20 principal held fast, and once he had tugged away the first twenty percent, the other eighty dutifully followed, revealing a clean pale ring around the branch.

He hung his yellow jacket from a branch like a flag hovering over his beautiful woodpile, then set out to try to retrace his steps. He found the clearing with the Horse Chestnut table top, so he knew that he was in the vicinity, and then tried to work his way backwards to where he had been before the encounter with Paulo.

His route had been random and unplanned. He remembered that he had circled and zig-zagged, so he circled and zig-zagged some more, this time in roughly the opposite direction. He stopped to take stock. He could clearly see a big imposing oak. He felt that it was looking down on him accusingly and he walked towards it putting his hands together as if praying "Sorry. I got distracted." He pointed to his hessian patch "This should make everything all right.

He touched the oak respectfully and then walked out from the trunk in search of the injured sapling, hoping that it was not too late to repair the damage he had caused. Stopping at an upright sapling he looked around, searching the circumference of the oak's canopy for its damaged offspring. Yet there was nothing, just a single sapling that had found all of the odds in its favour and managed to put down roots. Kneeling and looking at its base, he looked over to the mother oak and then back again. "This was it. This was the spot, but how..?"

The base of the sapling was in perfect condition. Shiny and smooth. No sign whatsoever of any damage or stress. He held the thin base in his fist as he had earlier in the day and gently pulsed his grip "One, two, three" he whispered then released his grip.

"I've fixed it. The little one, she's perfect again" scratching at his forehead he did a double take, then sat for a while examining the minute details of the palm of his hand.

Dugdale stood outside on the stone base that had once been the hard standing for the hermit's cabin and lit up a cigarette. He refused to stay in the cave listening to Paulo's abuse and left Marrielle inside making small talk.

Moonboots followed him out.

"You did right there Brian. Best just to walk away. The story's the important thing. Let's just wait for Christie to come back and stick to our plan."

There was a long drag of the cigarette.

"I felt like smacking him. Do you remember that time when he did the press briefing when Capriolo was 'too furious' to talk?"

"No."

"Well he did. He only had about 200 words of English then, but I made him sound like a tactical genius."

He feigned an over the top Italian accent "'We make good substitute.' That was it. That was all he said. Now listen to him all la-de-da and up his own arse."

Moonboots raised his index finger and tapped the side of his nose.

"Yes but, ask yourself, what's he doing in a cave reading books and drinking wine out of a crystal glass with a renegade goalkeeper? What's going on here Brian?"

This time a short, sharp draw on the cigarette preceded a quizzical look in the direction of Moonboots, and for a few seconds Dugdale held the pose.

"Shame The News of The World has gone. They'd have made a double page spread out of just that. But you're right, there's something odd here. We know Christie's gone a bit doolally, but you don't suppose they're er, you know, 'together' do you?"

Folding his arms, Moonboots looked towards the cave entrance and considered the question for a moment.

"I was just thinking that he might have been sent by Capriolo to bring him back. But Capriolo said he has no idea where Christie is."

"What did I say about him though? He leaves a lot of blank spaces. He might have just committed another sin of omission."

Walking across to Dugdale, Moonboots leaned on him shoulder to shoulder and placed his mouth close to his ear.

"Or . . . the two of them planned it, so that they could be together. Remember what Capriolo said about the whispers about Christie. Paulo must know about the whispers and he's sitting there like Pocahontas reading books? It's a bit suspect if you ask me Brian."

There was the sound of breaking twigs and a swishing of the undergrowth as Jonathan bounded into the clearing with a bright yellow bundle from which protruded twigs of all shapes and sizes. He frantically tipped the contents next to the hearth he had built, breathing deeply he paced about in an agitated state looking at the four faces as Marrielle and Paulo came to the mouth of the cave on hearing the commotion.

Marrielle was the first to speak as she gave him a look of concern.

"JC are you okay. You look a bit flustered."

He continued his pacing, still breathing heavily.

"Okay? Yes. I've just done something" he said looking up to the sky and pulsing his fists together three times.

"Is it something good or bad?" Marrielle said as she approached him and put her hands on his arms to try to calm him.

"It was bad. I shouldn't have done it. I don't know why I did it. Then it was good. It was more than good."

As if talking to a young boy who may be about to own up to a piece of mischief, Marrielle tried to sound caring and non-judgemental.

"Well? Would you like to tell us about it?"

Jonathan turned and walked in a circle and then stopped and swallowed hard. He looked at all four of them one by one.

"It's a miracle. I've done a miracle. I've just brought a tree back to life."

There was silence. Marrielle looked over to Paulo. Dugdale locked eyes with Moonboots and tilted his head in disbelief.

"This story just gets better and better. Get that Bentley on order Moonboots."

CHAPTER TWENTY-ONE
THE BIG IDEA

The fire danced gently throwing darting patterns of light and shade into the mouth of the cave. A blanket had been laid down alongside a couple of stumps next to length of tree trunk arranged a bit like a wooden three piece suite.

Paulo had put the maximum distance between himself and Dugdale so that they sat with the fire between them, catching glimpses of each other in between the ebb and flow of the flames. Moonboots sat on a stump next to Paulo, trying to douse his disdain for Dugdale, and next to him Marrielle and Jonathan occupied the blanket.

There was enough Aquavit left for everyone to have a shot and after a time, this and the soothing effect of the flames, relaxed everyone. An almost full moon hovered above them.

Moonboots tried to engage Paulo in conversation to ease the tension.

"See that moon Paulo? How many times would you have to fold a piece of paper for it to be thick enough to reach the moon do you think?"

Paulo eyed Moonboots suspiciously and gave him a long stare as though he had spotted a trap that had been laid for him, before giving a confident and knowing nod of the head.

"This is trick question. You are like your friend over there, always the trick question. Is not possible. I know it is physically impossible to fold a piece of paper more than six times. Even with a piece of paper the size of the Earth you would need to fold it probably a billion times to make it thick enough to reach the moon, and no matter how big the paper, it can only fold six times. So your question is bullshit."

This was a question Moonboots had posed many times before and he could not have been more delighted with Paulo's answer, providing him as it did, with the perfect opportunity to demonstrate his knowledge of logarithmic progression.

"You are right Paulo. Physically you can't fold the paper more than six times, but you can calculate its thickness for an infinite number of folds. Believe it or not, if you folded a piece of paper, any size, its thickness would reach the moon in just fifty turns of the page."

Jonathan sat up straight and laughed in disbelief.

"Piss off? A piece of paper's as thick as your fingernail. Fifty fingernails add up to about one centimeter. You're talking bollocks Moonboots."

Marrielle produced the pamphlet *The Wonders of the Edge*, unfolded it and laid it flat so that it became A4 size, and invited Moonboots to demonstrate his theory. First he

THE ART OF BEING ONE

explained that Jonathan's way of thinking was what was known as linear growth, adding one fingernail on top of another did produce a pile of fifty fingernails maybe a centimeter thick. Folding the paper though, resulted in the thickness doubling and doubling again with each fold, which had quite small effects with the first few folds, but enormous effects as the folding progressed. He folded the paper to show that it was already a centimeter thick at just six folds and then for Paulo's benefit showed that a seventh fold was not physically possible.

"You can work it all out yourself on paper. By the tenth fold the paper stack will be as high as a bus, so the eleventh fold takes you to the height of two buses. By the twentieth fold you've reached Mount Everest so in the next fold you are doubling Everests'. In just fifty folds you have reached the moon."

There was a look of confusion on Jonathan's face. He at once wanted to believe it, yet found the concept too incredible to be true. Moonboots noticing his interest picked him out for his standard follow up question.

"So JC. How many turns of the page would you need to go to the moon and back?"

Jonathan wriggled uncomfortably as the four looked at him expectantly.

"Well, it's got to be a hundred obviously."

Moonboots pursed his lips.

"Marrielle. What do you think?"

She had always disliked anything to do with numbers, and had a standing joke with her parents, giving the same answer whenever she was asked to calculate anything. She gave a childlike giggle.

"A zillion."

She giggled some more, whilst Moonboots gave an exaggerated tut.

"Paulo, would you care to advance your solution?"

"Is fifty-one."

With the raise of an eyebrow, Moonboots invited Dugdale to throw in his answer. Dugdale of course had heard all of this before, but went along with it anyway.

"I agree with Paulo. It's fifty-one."

Paulo's head retracted into his shoulders, and he looked over to the others.

"He agree with me? The man who writes fiction, finally recognizes fact?"

It took longer for Dugdale to scramble to his feet than it should have for him to look sufficiently threatening. He assembled his bulk and breathing heavily stared across the fire at Paulo.

"That's it. I'm not taking any more shit from you Paulo. I used to have to put up with it. I don't anymore. Show some respect yeah?"

"Respect? You make me want to spit."

Jonathan stood up and put his hand on Brian's shoulder.

"Sit down and calm down Brian. Paulo, don't you think you've done enough spitting for one day? Come on, let's try to get on shall we?"

The two eyed each other across the flames liked two scolded schoolboys, going along with what the teacher said but each feeling a deep sense of injustice.

"I don't get it Moonboots" Jonathan said "How can it be fifty-one. Surely it's a hundred?"

"Well imagine this piece of paper that is now so thick it has reached the moon. Every time you fold it, it's thickness doubles, so the fifty-first fold gives you twice the distance to the moon. The moon and back again."

Jonathan looked up at the moon and sat quietly for a moment trying to imagine this vast folded piece of paper stretching out into the heavens. His brow furrowed as in his mind he tried to fold the paper one more time imagining the doubling effect that Moonboots had described, wincing as if feeling the weight of the new paper fold land on the floor in front of him.

"Wow. If that's true that's amazing."

Bringing his hands together in the shape of a church steeple, Moonboots looked satisfied with the outcome of his little puzzle.

"It's a mathematical fact JC. Tomorrow, I'll bring a large sheet of paper and a pen if you like and I'll go through the equation with you."

"Yeah. Let's do that Moonboots. I'd like to see that." He looked towards the moon and nodded his head as if lost in a mental calculation.

Paulo's eyes watched the flickering flames of the fire. The constant waffle from Moonboots and the intermittent exchanges from the others seemed to get sucked away, first becoming muffled sound and then non-existent. Silence. The flames seemed to take him to another place. A place of calm. He thought about his life before he had married Gisa, before the bambinos came along. It was outwardly a good life being a young footballer in Italy, but there were always the jibes from the other lads that made things uncomfortable. Then he married the girl they all would have wanted and the wind-up merchants had nowhere to go with their wisecracks. That shut them up.

Yet one shaky façade had just been replaced with another. Fifteen years of hiding the truth from Gisa had taken its toll. Anxiety was a more or less constant companion. As each year went by he seemed to become more and more irritable and short tempered. He wondered if his anxiety transmitted to the players. What about the kids? Who wants a dad that's angry all of the time? There were laughs of course, but lately he'd found it hard to enjoy them, fearful that the conversation would turn to 'suspect' behaviour of some form or another. Even though the homophobic banter was not aimed at him directly, more and more he felt he could see veiled references.

He imagined a large pocket of black vapour assembling in his abdomen. As he breathed deeply inward, he saw the warmth of the flames go in and on the outward breath he imagined a quantity of black vapour being released. In time the darkness that had been in the pit of his stomach had been replaced by the light and heat of the fire giving Paulo the sensation of levitating slightly above the tree stump sat on.

"I think Paulo has found his place" Marrielle said gently nodding towards him. They watched for a while saying nothing until Paulo eventually looked up from the fire.

"I should go home. Gisa will be wondering where I am" he said, walking into the cave to collect his things and put them into his small knapsack. Jonathan followed him and placed a hand on his shoulder.

"Paulo. I don't know what any of this means yet. I just know I have to be here now. Don't betray me. Don't tell Capriolo where I am."

"Is difficult. We need to get back to normal. I suppose if I betray you, you betray me eh? An eye for an eye a tooth for a tooth, isn't that what they say? Maybe we are locked in our secret pact?" He yanked his head sideways in the direction of the cave entrance, placed his finger to his lips and whispered "Those two out there. They will betray you."

Jonathan pursed his lips "No. I'm getting to like those two. Moonboots goes on a bit, but he says some interesting stuff and Brian's, well, Brian's harmless."

"Did you ever meet a harmless journalist? He has only one thing on his mind. The story. You watch him like a hawk."

He held out his hand towards Jonathan "I thank you for listening to me. I don't know why I tell you these things, I never tell anyone."

Jonathan embraced Paulo in a strong unmistakably macho hug, and they each slapped each other's backs hard.

"It's going to be alright Paulo. Good things happen to good people don't they? We're both good people. I know you've got a duty to the gaffer and the others, but just give me a few days, yes?"

Paulo said his goodbyes to Marrielle and Moonboots and began to make his way along the path out of the clearing. He stopped, his shoulders dropped and he walked back a few paces.

"Brian. I sorry. These days I always seem to be angry. I don't want to be angry anymore."

They shook hands cautiously, and Paulo now looking more

relaxed offered to show Dugdale and Moonboots the way back to their budget hotel in the village.

After they had gone Marrielle placed a log on the fire and began to excite the flames using a wooden poker that was burned at one end.

"What are you thinking about JC, or shall I call you Jonathan like Paulo does?"

"You can call me either. I don't think my adventure has long left to run, so whatever."

She sat close to him on the blanket as he silently gazed up into the sky.

"So you didn't answer my question. What are you thinking about?"

He remained silent for a while and turned his gaze on the moon.

"I'm thinking about that. Fifty-one turns of a piece of paper."

CHAPTER TWENTY-TWO
RABBITS IN THE BUSH

It was cold in the cave that first morning. The small shaft of sunlight which had begun encroaching into the entrance did little to lift the chill. Marrielle wrapped herself around Jonathan and felt the harsh, wiry rub of his beard against her soft cheek.

"Good morning Mr. JC Jonathan or whatever you're called" she said tweeking the short hairs of his beard.

He squeezed Marrielle hard "You can call me anything. It doesn't matter, I don't know who I am or where I'm going, or why. I'm lost."

She made a gentle circling motion on his chest with her fingers. "Halmund always used to say things like 'Get lost because when you get lost you find yourself.' He would agree with what you are doing."

Jonathan squeezed her hand "Are you sure you and Halmund aren't an item?"

She laughed, rubbed her forehead into his beard and then laughed again. "No. Halmund was the most magnificent man I ever met, that's all. He was the greatest fiddler that ever lived, philosopher, guru, silversmith, whatever. I was his apprentice. He taught me everything, everything about the Hardanger and everything about how to live."

She'd spent ten years with Halmund Bjørgum. There had been a great leaving party at Narvic when she set off for the tiny settlement on Sonjefjord that was the Hardanger fiddle equivalent of Motown. Halmund knew that Marrielle played well just by hearing the tapes that Mo Stordhal had sent. When she arrived at the his small collection of barns, sheds and workshops he had told her that before she could become a truly great player, she must truly find herself.

"All good fiddlers can play all the notes" he had said "The truly great fiddlers play *above* the notes. Something from deep within their soul makes contact with the fretwork and something magical happens. The gates of heaven begin to open."

She would have stayed longer, but Halmund felt the time had come for Marrielle to experience the wider world and as he put it "Deepen her soul."

She smiled at the memory. "Another one of his sayings was "Draw your life in pencil, then you can change it if you don't like it." That's one for you JC. That's what you're doing."

"I don't think so. My life's drawn in pen. The fixture lists, the training schedules, the sponsorship duties, the press calls,

THE ART OF BEING ONE

the rest periods. Always sacrificing myself for the 'good of the team'. I'm stuck. Here I can just be me. Whoever that is. I'm not one of eleven any more. I'm just one."

She held his chin and made him look at her in the eyes "So if you draw yourself in pencil, what does it look like?"

"I don't know. But maybe that's what I should do" He kissed her lips "Thank you Halmund."

The Turkish waitress couldn't help but smile every time she looked at the 'odd couple' that had been seen wandering about the village. Sitting at a pavement table surrounded by waif like women, and men in business suits, they looked like they could have descended from another planet. Dugdale with his gut pressing hard against the table edge, and Moonboots with his trademark boots stretched out so that she had to keep stepping over them.

Dugdale nodded in her direction "I think she fancies you Moonboots."

Moonboots concurred, "She keeps on smiling at me."

"See. There she goes again. You're in there Moonboots."

He cleared his throat nervously "Well, some women like the older man. It's intelligence you see. It's an aphrodisiac."

"They reckon that this areas full of gold diggers. She's probably worked out what you're worth already. How much is your benefit payment these days?" he laughed and gently punched Moonboots on the arm.

Moonboots smiled back at the waitress "Probably a bit more than your non-existent redundancy cheque."

"Alright Moonboots we both could use a payday. The big money is in Christie. We need him signed up, legally like, for me to write his exclusive story. Papers will pay for the exclusive from the horse's mouth."

The waitress interrupted placing a gentle hand on Moonboots shoulder. "Would you like another coffee? I like your boots by the way. They are . . . unusual." She cleared away the cups and shared a laugh with another waitress on the way back to the kitchen.

"I like it up here Brian. We probably look quite bohemian to them. She probably thinks I'm a poet or something like that. I reckon we could score here."

"Moonboots, she must be all of twenty-three. Come on. How do we get Christie signed up, that's all we should be thinking about."

Moonboots put on what he thought was an intellectual face, involving some rubbing of the chin with the palm of his hand and then he folded his left arm across his chest and pinched the top of his nose with his right hand. He checked to see if the waitress had noticed him. She hadn't.

"It's the old 'Bird in the hand' issue Brian. We could take the money and run now, probably we could get pissed for a few weeks and that would be it. Or we could hold out for the big one – but risk losing out."

The waitress returned and placed two cappuccinos carefully on the table. Moonboots lightly stroked her arm.

"Would you mind answering a question? he said.

She removed her arm and dusted it with her other hand, "That depends. What kind of question?"

"Are you familiar with the old English saying 'A bird in the hand is worth two in the bush'?"

She smiled broadly "Yes we do the same thing in Turkey only with rabbits not birds."

"Good. Which is better, a rabbit in the hand or two in the bush?"

There was a pause whilst she stared into the middle distance "It is for everyone to decide, but with a rabbit in the hand I would still be in my small village in Turkey. Here I am in a beautiful place surrounded by beautiful people, so for me it is two in the bush. I take a chance." She wheeled off smartly and disappeared into the kitchen.

"There's no right answer Brian. We can be 'Kings for a Day' back in the pub or we can change our lives. I vote for the two rabbits in the bush."

On the other side of the street, Marrielle stood with her embroidered canvas bag over her shoulder trying to catch their attention. She waved and let out a high-pitched "Cuckoo."

Dugdale looked up "Birds, rabbits, now cuckoos. Pull up another chair. She's coming over."

There was warmth in the way that they greeted each other. In a short time they had driven up from the Midlands, 'pixie hunted' together and spent a weird night around a campfire with a latter day hermit and an irritable Italian. Moonboots caught the eye of the Turkish waitress, who signaled with her finger, then asked Samu, her male colleague to take the order.

Marrielle slipped the strap of her canvas bag over her head and sat down. They reflected on the events of the previous night and laughed about Paulo.

"He saw something in the fire" she said, "I've seen that kind of thing before. For ten thousand years we humans looked closely at fire, then they gave us central heating and we stopped looking. There are things in the fire that can tell us about ourselves if we can be bothered to look. Paulo looked."

The coffee came. She took a sip and then looked at Dugdale hard.

"JC knows who you are Brian. He wants to be at one with himself for a bit. Are you going to betray him to your newspaper friends?"

He rocked back in his chair surprised to be singled out so abruptly.

"Hang on Marrielle. I don't have any newspaper friends. Not anymore. Well probably not for a long time. We like the lad don't we Moonboots?"

Moonboots placed a reassuring hand between Marrielle's shoulder blades and gently ran it in a circle a few times.

"He's a nice fella, but he can't live in a cave forever. Sooner or later he's going to have to come out. I mean come out of the cave. Well, maybe he's going to have to 'come out' as well."

Marrielle looked quizzical "What do you mean 'come out' as well'?"

Moonboots let out a long sigh as if he had been withholding a secret for years "Well, it's come to our attention that there have been a few whispers about, you know, his sexuality let's say."

She squeezed his hand and laughed, "Let's say those whispers were wrong" she winked across the table at Dugdale "There's no way on earth that man is gay" exaggerating her stare to make sure that her point had hit home.

Like two schoolboys they looked at each other, looked away from the table, one coughed one wriggled and both flushed slightly. Dugdale slurped at his coffee. "The thing is Marrielle, the papers will write what they want, I can go along with Paulo to an extent. It's better that someone he trusts writes things from his perspective, that's all."

"He wants to meet with you later. Both of you. Moonboots you must bring the equation you talked of, the moon thing, and Brian he wants you to help him with something. Come on, he may only have a few days of freedom, give the guy a break eh?"

She pulled out a shopping list that she had drawn up with Jonathan and read it out loud.

Large sheets of paper
Soft pencil(s)
Woodworking tools of some kind
probably chisels and a mallet
a saw if possible
Marmite
Some sort of paraffin heater or similar
A calculator
A compass
Pontefract cakes – in Mrs Beatties – middle shelf behind the counter.

"If you want to betray him go ahead. You stay here. If you want to help him then come with me and we will see if we can find this stuff"

They looked at each other unsure of what they should do. "What the hell are Pontefract cakes?" Moonboots asked.

"Little black circles" Dugdale answered "They look like congealed blobs of Marmite. Probably taste the same too."

She folded up the list and popped it back into her bag. "So, what is it to be? Do you stay or do you come?"

"We're coming" Dugdale said "But hang on Marrielle. What's in it for you? What do you get out of all of this?"

"I don't know what's in it for me Brian" she said throwing her bag over her shoulder and looking up in the direction of the Edge. She feigned a mysterious voice "Perhaps I will deepen my soul and then I will play above the notes"

"So do you come?" she said walking out onto the pavement.

"We're coming. I'll get the bill" Moonboots said.

Dugdale stood with Marrielle and waited "That's not like him" he said as they watched Moonboots approach the till.

The little Turkish waitress walked to the kitchen and closed the door.

CHAPTER TWENTY-THREE
PAULO THROUGH THE WINDOW

Paulo spent a sleepless night. He was alone. It had been some time now since he and Gisa had slept in the same bed. There were the post Cup Final celebrations when all of the wives would come and it couldn't be avoided, but even on holiday with the kids they would arrange for twin beds. As far as the kids were concerned, Papa needed to rest properly so he could look after the team and Mamma didn't want to be disturbed when he got home late from night games and away matches.

There had been no great discussion about it. She had just suggested that he might feel better sleeping in his own room. He agreed it might be worth a try. It just went on from there until it became the normal routine and neither of them really wanted to analyse why. The truth was he preferred to have his own space. He slept better, but this night sleeping was not easy.

He knew that he had a loyalty as part of Capriolo's inner circle, yet he had shared a secret with Jonathan and been welcomed rather than shunned. It was hard to know what to do and the more he mulled over the options and possible consequences, the more the knot in the centre of his abdomen tightened and expanded.

He had reached into his draw where he kept a batch of Men's Health magazines, purely for professional reasons as he had told Gisa, and rummaged around for a feature he had read recently about how to unlock the chakras. He'd even toyed with the idea that he might introduce a more spiritual dimension to match preparation, but his talk of energy flows and universal balance had not been well received when he raised it casually one day when Capriolo had been holding court in Vincenzo's. He reminded himself of the seven chakras and tried to breathe deeply imagining an energy force running from the top to the bottom of his body. But the energy flows kept hitting a roadblock smack bang in the centre of his body, and the knot in his stomach tightened some more.

In the morning Gisa handed him an expresso and continued to get the kids ready for school. She'd stopped asking where he'd been or what time he came home. When the men were together at Vincenzo's or one of their houses, they would often talk late into the night, especially if it was the night before a non-training day. That's how she liked to think of it anyway. It suited both of them. He didn't have to explain or apologise.

His eyes were stinging and his legs leaden as he made his way down the high street towards Vincenzo's. In the distance he could see Marrielle with Dugdale and Moonboots walking in his direction. The last thing he needed.

Instinctively he wheeled in through the door of the Oxfam bookshop and began to bury himself behind the shelves, playing for time to allow the threesome to pass by. He browsed the books for a while, flitting about randomly from shelf to shelf, opening the odd book here and there until he fell upon one that caught his eye, and sat down in a wicker chair that had been set up by a small coffee table so that browsers could settle for a while. Then lost himself in the rhythm of Auden's *Night Mail*. Gently his head moved backwards and forwards as he read the poem in the rhythm of an express train. The aching in his body began to lift, though the tightness in the gut remained.

He felt an urge to look towards the window. Capriolo was standing motionless, expressionless looking in on Paulo. The two locked eyes, but there was no acknowledgement from his boss, who turned on his heel and continued in the direction of Vincenzo's.

The aching in his body that had begun to ebb away flowed back with such force that he felt himself sink deeper into the chair as if he had just been handed a substantial weight, forcing himself up, he headed for Vincenzo's.

Capriolo had already begun talking through his thoughts

on team selection, asking for updates on injuries and the fitness of particular players and then interrupted his flow. "Paulo are you all right?"

Paulo flushed "Of course, why shouldn't I be?"

"You look like shit that's all."

"I didn't sleep good, tomorrow I be fine."

Little Roberto nudged Marco with his elbow, knowing that he was playing a dangerous game, but feeling that he was seated far enough away to be able to eke out a little revenge for Paulo pushing him over last time they met.

"Perhaps he is pining for Jonathan?" he said and then pouted his lips causing a ripple of laughter around the table.

There was no time for Capriolo to admonish Little Roberto and this time Paulo was in no mood to be held back by anybody. He flipped the table over causing coffee cups and their contents to fly in all directions, before launching himself at Little Roberto and pinning him to the floor landing three serious punches to the face. A rugby scrum ensued as people began trying to pull Paulo away but he seemed oblivious to his surroundings and the more they tried to hold him back, the more frenzied he became.

Capriolo himself stepped up to try to calm Paulo, who was being held tightly by two colleagues, only to be head butted hard on the bridge of the nose and sent tumbling over a stainless steel chair onto the floor.

As everybody moved to help Capriolo up onto his feet, Paulo almost took the door off its hinges as he stormed out into the street.

Vincenzo carefully eyed up the door, rubbing his hands

across the hinges as if they had been part of Paulo's frenzied attack. Gently he pushed the door into its frame, clicked on the Yale lock and turned his open sign to closed.

From his back room he brought out a bottle of brandy and five glasses and sat with the group as they fussed around the two injured men. Capriolo downed his brandy in one go, which everybody took to be a signal to do the same.

"What's going on with him? Something is not right" said Capriolo holding a napkin up to the bridge of his nose, to mop up a small trickle of blood. "Has he said anything to any of you?"

Little Roberto fiddled with his nose, worrying that it might be broken "He's got it coming to him, the mad bastard."

"We stop talking like this. What is happening to us? We stay together. We have to ask why he behave like this. Is everything all right at home, Gisa, the kids?"

There was silence. Capriolo continued.

"I will go and find him. Calm him down. Little Roberto, when I bring him back, you must shake hands, say you're sorry."

"No. No. No. He must apologise to me. Even then I no want to shake hands with him, he's mental" he said, standing up at the table and giving Capriolo a defiant stare.

Capriolo spoke slowly almost in a whisper.

"You shake his hand. Is simple."

Little Roberto made for the door, lifted the latch and turned to spit on the floor.

"I spit in his face. The ugly bastard" he said slamming the door hard.

For a second time Vincenzo carefully examined his door,

then flipped the latch back down again. He raised his arms in desperation "If this carry on, I will be running the team."

Capriolo had to admit to himself that the odds of someone else running the team had just shortened. Maybe it was true. Perhaps his two wildcards Fanni and Mushi were more trouble than they were worth.

CHAPTER TWENTY-FOUR
DRAW YOUR LIFE IN PENCIL

Paulo was breathless by the time he reached The Hermit. He'd begun running hard when his feet hit the pavement outside Vincenzo's, partly to distance himself from the others, but also to try to extinguish the anger that was still surging through his veins.

His heart pounded as he raced up the steep rise of Squirrels Jump and then out onto the earthen pathways that zig-zagged across The Edge, so that his lungs wanted to burst.

Jonathan was busy clearing rocks and stones from what was left of The Hermit's garden, with a view to bringing it back to life should he be able to acquire some suitable tools. He'd assembled three separate pyramid-like piles. Rocks the size of a hand or bigger on one pile, those the size of golf balls on another, and next to this, everything he found that was smaller. The small rocks took the greatest time to assemble, and these formed the biggest pile, but time didn't seem to matter anymore and he enjoyed the bending and stretching almost as much as the unexpected pleasure he had derived from creating order out of chaos.

The pleasant calm was interrupted as Paulo burst into The Hermit and finally recovered sufficient composure to speak.

"I'm finished Jonathan. I just totally lost it with Little Roberto and the Gaffer. Left them lying on the floor in Vincenzo's."

He walked up and down and from side to side around the clearing, he pulled at his hair, clenched his fists and banged his forehead with the palm of his hand.

Jonathan sat down on a stump and watched the angst ridden Italian for a while hoping that stillness would exude a degree of calm in his direction.

"Do nothing Paulo. Do nothing, say nothing. Let's just be calm. Behave ourselves with as much dignity as we can for as long as we can and in time the truth will be seen."

It didn't calm Paulo, and he clenched his fists as he spoke through gritted teeth.

"I can't let the truth be seen. My life will be over."

"Sit down Paulo."

Paulo sat on a tree stump opposite, laid his arms on his thighs and slumped his head down towards his knees.

"I'm in a mess. Sometimes I just feel like topping myself."

"When you create a new space, new people step into it.

That's what I did when I walked off the pitch. That's what you can do" said Jonathan.

Paulo lifted his head slightly and thought for a moment. "Jonathan, where you get this shit from?"

"Halmund."

"Who the Hell is Halmund? That prick with the stupid boots?"

Jonathan smiled "No. That's Moonboots, and he's not such a prick. Halmund was Marrielle's teacher. He came to me in a dream and told me that."

Paulo sat up. Then stood and walked a few paces away.

"Are you listening to yourself Jonathan? He came to you in a dream? You've lost it amici."

"Are you listening to yourself Paulo? You've been living a lie for twenty-five years, now you've thumped Little Roberto and the gaffer? There's no way things can ever be the same. It's a chance to create a new space."

"There can be no new space. It's better that I end it. Walk in front of a train or something like the German keeper did."

Jonathan put an arm around his neck and pulled Paulo towards him wrapping him in a great bear hug.

"Stay here for a bit mate. Let your head clear. We'll work it all out."

Dugdale and Moonboots stopped in their tracks as they entered The Hermit followed closely by Marrielle. The pair exchanged glances, but said nothing as Jonathan and Paulo stood locked together in what seemed to them to be a passionate embrace.

There was a moment of discomfort as Jonathan released Paulo from his grip. He held his arms out wide.

"Paulo's got a few issues at work. He's going to stay up here for a bit. We're going to create a new space and new people will step into it."

Dugdale and Moonboots were unsure what this meant, but Marrielle pushed in between them smiling.

"That's what Halmund always used to say."

"I know" said Jonathan "Come on let's see what you were able to get from the shopping list."

Marrielle organized the tipping out of the contents from the bags they were each carrying. She was excited and keen to show Jonathan each item individually. The Marmite and the Pontefract cakes had been easy to get. The paraffin heater not so, but they had managed to find a modest calor gas heater in one of the charity shops, it had no gas bottle, but Marrielle felt sure that the gas bottle from the stove in Clementine would fit and promised to go and get it later so that they could test it out.

The charity shop had also provided the calculator and the compass, the craft shop had been a good source for the paper and pencils, but they had had no joy with the mallet, chisels or the saw. Marrielle suggested a trip to a DIY store, maybe in Macclesfield, and Jonathan asked if he might add some gardening tools to the list. He had done as much as he could on clearing the garden by hand, now a trowel and a spade of some kind would be useful, maybe even some seeds.

"What are we supposed to do now?" Dugdale asked "With all of this, this ... paraphernalia?"

Jonathan looked to Marrielle "Tell them. Tell them what Halmund said. You know about drawing your life in pencil."

Paulo grimaced.

THE ART OF BEING ONE

"Don't make funny faces Paulo" said Marrielle. "Many people draw their life in pen. Much better Halmund said, to draw it in pencil, then if you don't like it you can rub it out."

Jonathan picked up the pack of Cumberland Graphite 2B pencils and counted them.

"There are six here, and five of us. Somebody else must be coming into our new space."

He gave everyone a pencil and tore off five sheets of A3 paper from an artist's pad, handing one to everybody.

"Let's do it" he said.

"Do what?" Moonboots asked.

"Let's draw our lives in pencil eh? Imagine that you could just get rid of your existing life – the life we've probably drawn in pen – and replace it with a new life that we could draw in pencil and not be stuck with it if we didn't like it. Just draw it. What would it look like?"

Dugdale leaned over and pushed his mouth close to Moonboots ear "He's lost the flipping plot."

Moonboots nodded "Yes, but what a story this is gonna be. Did you see them cuddling?"

Jonathan began to sketch something on his paper, and Marrielle delightedly began a doodle on hers. Paulo was frozen to the spot.

"I not happy with this. This doesn't feel right. We are men, we just have to get on with things. Why we do this?"

"That's just it Paulo" said Jonathan "We end up trying to make our lives work, when maybe it would be better to invent a new life. Look, nobody's watching. Let's all find our own space in the forest and do our drawings. We don't have to show each other. What have we got to lose?"

Marrielle jumped up and prodded Dugdale and Moonboots. "Great. Come on you two, let's go and find a place."

Paulo eyed Jonathan suspiciously and slowly stood up holding his paper in one hand and his pencil in the other.

"Okay. I do something, but I not show anyone."

They split up with their papers and pencils eventually straggling back to the clearing one by one. Dugdale and Moonboots walked back together, both feeling slightly embarrassed that they had managed to draw something on the paper.

Moonboots prodded Dugdale, "Let's have a look at what you drew."

"It's personal" he said "Why what did you draw?"

Moonboots rolled it up into a scroll "This Brian, is for my eyes only. A blueprint for a new future when we get this story sold."

Marrielle appeared next and stood in the clearing holding up her drawing. She smiled as she admired it.

"Anyone want to see what I drew?"

Dugdale looked nervous "Er, we don't have to show them. Those were the rules. Jonathan said, didn't you Jonathan?"

"That's right" he said "And thanks. You used my real name"

Marrielle persisted "Yes that's right, he said you don't *have* to show them, that doesn't mean that you can't."

Paulo slowly walked back into the clearing and handed Jonathan his pencil.

"Where's your drawing?" Asked Moonboots.

"Is here" Paulo said, slapping his breast pocket which was sealed with a press stud. "I no show it no one."

"All right, well you can all look at mine if you want"

Marrielle said, laying her drawing on a tree stump and inviting everyone to gather around.

The picture had a cartoon feel about it. There was clearly a caricature of Marrielle standing outside her van, but she had a funnel coming out of her head, with a big question mark at the top of the funnel. A rope ladder wound its way out of the side door of Clementine coming to rest on what looked to be the Earth, landing in a spot marked 'Christiana'.

"That's shit" said Dugdale spluttering with contempt for Marrielle's drawing, but she remained smiling.

"It might be shit to you Brian, but to me it represents a beautiful life. Why don't you show us yours?"

"I refer you to Jonathan's earlier ruling. Nobody has to show if they don't want to. I don't want to" he said taking on the air of a bar room barrister.

Paulo examined the drawing closely, silently following each line, frowning every so often.

"Is nice" he said "Naïve, like a child, but I like it. What is the reason for this question mark? It mean you are confused yes?"

"No" she said, "It just means I'm very curious and being curious is going to take me somewhere."

"Why Christiana?" asked Jonathan.

"That's where I grew up. It's a sort of a hippie commune where the normal rules don't apply. Maybe my drawing is telling me that I need to go back there."

"You didn't say it was called Christiana" Jonathan said, standing up as if he had somehow been offended.

"Didn't I? But I told you all about it, the Narvic Bar & Grill, Moe Stordhal and the tapes he sent to Halmund Bjørgum?"

"Yes, but you didn't say it was called Christiana", he reiterated as he turned and walked into the cave.

Marrielle shrugged and looked over to Paulo who was still studying her drawing intently.

"So what is the drawing telling you about your life?" he asked.

She put her index finger up to her chin and thought for a moment.

"I think" she pondered some more "It's telling me that I like my life a lot, but now I think something is pulling me home, back to Christiana."

She picked up her drawing and ran her finger along a rope ladder that led to Christiana then furled it into a scroll and slipped it into her shoulder bag. She rubbed Dugdale's arm.

"Okay. Brian I think we know where you stand on sharing." He nodded and grunted. "Anyone else want to share? Moonboots? Paulo?"

Paulo fiddled with the press-stud button on his breast pocket and looked over to Moonboots, who looked over to Dugdale "I'm with Brian on this, I think its personal and should stay that way." Paulo quickly slipped his fingers away from his pocket and muttered "Si."

"That's fine" said Marrielle, then she turned towards the cave entrance. "Jonathan, do you want to share what's in your picture?"

There was no answer. Jonathan lay on top of the quilt covering his bed of vegetation and stared at his Travelcard, once again running his index finger along the tear stained letter 'T' that had mutated into the sign of a cross.

"Are you okay?" said Marrielle "You're looking at that Travelcard again?"

He turned onto his side and looked in her direction.

"It comforts me."

"Why, what made you uncomfortable? Me talking about my picture?"

"No. It was that place you mentioned. Christiana. I think I went there in a dream."

CHAPTER TWENTY-FIVE
PETE

Paulo walked behind Jonathan as he fiddled with his compass and made pencil marks on his A3 pad. The Italian looked around self-consciously even though there was no one around to witness what it was that they were doing.

"Jonathan, this no seem right to me. What are we doing? We are two grown men."

The two grown men were walking backwards and forwards along the lesser known tracks of The Edge, identifying what they thought were landmarks, drawing little symbols, whilst all the while trying to do something with the compass. Neither of them was quite sure what they were doing with the compass, except they knew that all maps were orientated towards the North, so they annotated each of their symbols according to its geographical orientation, hoping that when they came to produce a cleaned up version of the map, everything would fall into place. Jonathan knew that they could always ask Moonboots for advice, but that was something he would only want to do as a last resort.

"I'll tell you what we're doing Paulo. We're fulfilling a small part of my 'drawn in pencil' life. I just want to make a map."

There was a puzzled look on Paulo's face "Why Jonathan? Why you want to make this map?"

"Do I have to have a reason? I could have made a map any time I wanted in my old 'drawn in pen' life. But you know what? I never did. It never even crossed my mind. When I drew myself a new life I thought about the things I loved, things other than football, and I've always loved maps, but I've never made one so I thought well while I'm here, why not?"

There was a sadness about Paulo as he leaned against a smoothed over sandstone boulder. "You have fallen out of love with football?"

Jonathan looked around to be sure he could not be overheard and then looked to the ground and spoke quietly "I'm not sure. I think I'll always love the game in a way, but I think I've fallen out of love with the whole circus, the people, the things they stand for."

A pair of hikers looking like a husband and wife, ascended a rough-hewn rock staircase onto the track now blocked by Jonathan and Paulo. The man leaned his Nordic walking sticks against the boulder that Paulo was leaning on and they all exchanged greetings before performing what looked like a delicate dance to enable the couple to pass by.

Paulo remained staring into the distance from his sandstone boulder.

"I think I have" he said.

"Have what?"

"I think I've fallen out of love with everything. The game, the people, my wife. My life even. It's all shit."

"You just 'come out' mate" Jonathan said trying to make light of it "I know it sounds a bit, you know, a bit simplistic when I say that, but do you want to live a lie all of your life? Don't you want to be true to yourself?"

They tried to imagine the scenario where Paulo made his secret public. Since the homophobia ban, players tended to keep their thoughts largely to themselves, but Jonathan had remembered a discussion with, give or take a few, the same group of players that they both worked with now. There was a bit of a debate about what would happen if a player 'came out'. A few of the lads had gone along the route that it wouldn't really matter. Then someone pointed out about female linesmen "Do they share the same showers as the male referee?" someone asked. Of course they didn't, they had to have separate facilities.

Taking that argument further someone put forward the notion of a man playing for a ladies football team. Suppose they all shared the same showers? The question was asked if it was feasible for a straight man sharing a shower not to be attracted to or become aroused by one or more of his female teammates. There was no need for a vote, there was unanimous agreement that it was impossible. Therefore, the logic went, it would be impossible for a gay player to share the showers with everyone else. He would have to have separate facilities, he wouldn't be part of the team, he would be a separate entity.

Many doubted that there could be such a thing as a gay footballer, but if the statistics were to be believed, there must be some. It was hard to know who was playing to the crowd and who was genuinely intolerant but everyone was in no doubt that their dressing room was for heterosexuals only. Then the homophobia ban came in and everybody stopped talking about it. That didn't mean that their views had changed.

"And" Jonathan added, "You're not a player. The homophobia policy will protect you from abuse or unfair treatment, that's what it's there for."

"You think that shitty piece of paper changes anything? Come on, you are forgetting that I was a player too. I know how they think. Maybe they can't say it openly anymore, but their thinking hasn't changed. I would lose my authority and become the butt of their ridiculous jokes. They remind me of schoolboys sometimes."

"There's got to be a way out Paulo" Jonathan said tearing another piece of paper from his pad. He drew a circle in the middle and wrote the word 'Paulo' inside. "Why don't we see the problem as a map. Imagine you've been lost for a long time, lost in a kind of shitty wilderness that people looking at you thought was a paradise. Just like me. Let's fill in all the big landmarks, the obstacles, you know, stuff to be avoided. Then let's find a way out. Navigate like. It's like Halmund said 'Sometimes you have to get lost in order to find yourself'."

Paulo looked at the circle with his name in it and then looked at Jonathan "I getting a bit pissed off with this Halmund guy."

"There's no rush Paulo, but sooner or later you've got to address it. All I'm saying is that up here it's like we are separate from the world. It's a bit like we're in a helicopter looking down at it all. Now we can see the beauty in our lives as well as all the shit. We're in a position to sort the beauty from the shit. Why not?"

Paulo pushed back against the sandstone boulder, grimaced and slapped Jonathan's arm.

"Look you talk some shit sometimes, but there is some sense amongst your shit. Stop talking. I said I would help you with your little map didn't I? Isn't that enough? And anyway, isn't the idea of a goalkeeper making maps a bit 'suspect'?"

He caught Jonathan's eye and smiled. They both let out a snort of laughter and continued down the track letting out further minor eruptions of laughter along the way.

With the map taking shape, Paulo beckoned Jonathan towards a tree stump just off the track and suggested that he lay it down so that they could review it properly. For someone who made out that he had little interest in making the 'little map', Paulo seemed to want to argue the toss about every small thing. Jonathan engaged him in debates about whether The Beacon should be shown at forty-five degrees from Stormy Point or the correct orientation of Goldenstone. He'd seen this behaviour in Paulo before when they had been on the training pitch. He could not simply accept an idea, he had to argue it this way and that, often making a drama out of what seemed like fairly trivial points, but he always seemed happier with an idea or suggestion if he had first tried to destroy it before putting it back together again. This he did with the map, and after a few crossings out and promises from Jonathan that the next draft would take into account one or other of his suggestions, Paulo declared that they had the makings of what could be a good little map.

Just to test the idea that they believed they had made a 'good and true' map, they began to chart alternative ways to go back to The Hermit. Again Paulo saw it as a challenge and felt he had to oppose Jonathan's suggestion and make the case for his own.

Tiring of appeasing the Italian and feeling his own competitive instincts kicking in, Jonathan held fast to his view of the preferred route back.

"Look Paulo, whose map is this?"

"It is both of us. Ours. We both make it remember? If it had not been for me it would look ridiculous. It was all out of proportion, and that quarry over there was pointing the wrong way. If it comes to the crunch I would say it is 60:40 my map."

"No way Paulo"

"Yes way, Jonathan. Is 60:40 or nothing."

They stared at each other in silence for a while each wondering how far they wanted to escalate this dispute. The silence was invaded by a faint humming noise somewhere in the distance and both of them tilted their heads inquisitively and looked at each other.

"Can you hear that?" Jonathan asked Paulo.

"I think it is some machine. Maybe woodcutters getting ready to fell some trees."

Jonathan stood up and grabbed the map. Paulo looked offended "Hey where you go with my 60 per cent?"

"Come on, let's mark their position on the map, then later we can come back and get some of the offcuts for the fire."

Hunching their bodies they walked as quietly as they could towards the sound, until gradually it became louder. Their strides deliberate and long like children trying to walk tiptoed, looking backwards and forwards at each other as the noise grew louder, whispering little instructions as if there was every chance that the games teacher was about to catch them smoking.

Through a screen of trees they could see what appeared to be a giant slab of butter in a clearing. This it seemed was the source of the mechanical droning that they had heard. Paulo was the first to peer through the trees.

He turned to Jonathan "It's just a battered old car. Probably dumped by some kids" he whispered.

Now Jonathan peered through the trees to see a rusted and dented mustard coloured Skoda with its windows fogged up. A green garden hose ran from the exhaust pipe and was wedged in between the front passenger side window that was not completely closed.

"Shit Paulo, I think there's someone in there."

Both burst through the tree screen, and Paulo frantically pulled at the driver's side door then the passenger side door. Locked. He could see the outline of a young man lying down at forty-five degrees with the driver's seat reclined. He again tried to pull the driver's side door open yanking at it with as much force as he could yield.

Jonathan, after an initial surge of adrenaline found himself for some reason adopting his familiar goalkeepers 'ready position'. It was as if everything slowed down in his mind and ignoring Paulo's frantic efforts to free the passenger he calmly walked to the exhaust pipe and pulled off the green hose. Then, pushing Paulo to one side, he carefully balanced on his left leg and brought down three hammer blows with his right, shattering the driver's window into a thousand shards of glass.

Reaching inside, Paulo flipped the catch to unlock the door and wrestled out the semi-conscious body of a pale, spotty young man, clad in a crumpled maroon shell suit. He spread him out on the soft woodland floor and began pumping at his lungs to clear them of fumes, then expertly, gave the boy mouth to mouth resuscitation, the way he had tried to do unsuccessfully the day Floren Vallee had collapsed on the training pitch three years earlier. He had never recovered and Paulo fought with all his might to try to make sure he didn't fail a second time.

"Keep going Paulo, he can only have been in there two minutes or so"

Paulo didn't respond, and instead gave his full concentration to filling the boys lungs with clean air, until the lad, still looking shocked and dazed lay there panting of his own accord, his eyes barely open. When his eyes opened wider he turned his head towards Paulo.

"You should have just left me alone. I'd be gone by now if it wasn't for you."

Paulo smiled gently "Is nothing. I do it for anyone."

"I wasn't thanking you, you twat. I wanted to be gone. Why do you think I was in there?"

Almost in a reflex reaction, Paulo's arm raised and his hand flattened as if he was about to issue a firm slap to the boy's face. Jonathan caught Paulo by the wrist.

"Hang on Paulo. Cool it, the lad's not thinking straight. What's your name mate? What's going on?"

"Do you think we should call the police, get him to a hospital?" Paulo asked.

Jonathan was about to nod. It was, of course, the sensible, responsible thing to do, and then he stopped himself.

"If we do that though, we'll have to explain who we are, what we were doing here."

There was a look of mild disgust on Paulo's face.

"That's not going to look good. Two men who have disappeared, making a map together and sharing a cave."

"Not good" said Jonathan. "You gonna be okay mate?" he asked the lad.

"I'd rather not be here if that's what you're asking" he said sullenly.

"You're young mate. What's so bad that made you want to top yourself? You can talk about it if you want. We won't judge you."

The lad snorted heavily several times and silent tears ran down his cheeks as he lost himself in his own thoughts staring straight ahead as if watching a re-run of whatever events had led up to him lying in a battered car in the woods with a hosepipe attached to the exhaust.

Squeezing his arm hard, Jonathan stood up.

"Look. Take your time. Whenever you're ready mate. We'll try to help you if we can."

The lad raised his head.

"Nobody can help me."

Paulo emerged from the woods holding a piece of paper. "You dropped the map" he shouted "I rescued it from over there."

He folded it in four, slid it into the breast pocket of his jacket, and then looking triumphant, popped the press-stud firmly down until it gave a little click.

CHAPTER TWENTY-SIX
TEACUPS

In the world of football management 'throwing the teacups' was considered a fine art. There were times when an inspirational pep talk would motivate the team; other times when a gentle word in the ear of a player or two would do the trick; and then there were times when the manager had to metaphorically and sometimes literally throw the teacups against the dressing room wall.

Roberto Capriolo was one of those managers who thought carefully about how he behaved in front of his players. His view was if that you were always throwing the teacups, players became immune to bursts of anger. If they simply brushed off your outburst by saying "He's always like that" it ruled out one of the techniques for getting the desired response, that extra one percent of effort or application.

He could throw the teacups with the best of them when

he wanted to. He even practised when nobody was around just so that he could get the angle right to ensure that the smash produced the exact amount of drama. This was important to him. A cup that hit the wall and landed without a smash like a dead squash ball would make him appear weak. It would dilute the effect that he wanted to have on the rare occasions when he felt the need to bully his players.

They were rare occasions too. He didn't keep a tally of how many teacups he had destroyed in the name of motivation, but he tried to keep it to one or two mock incontrollable outbursts of fury each season.

There was nothing mock or rehearsed about the throwing of the teacups when Little Roberto was summoned to his office. Roberto Capriolo was so incensed he threw four teacups, the sugar bowl and the coffee pot at his office wall narrowly missing the head of his miniature namesake. With nothing left to throw, he hammered both his fists hard on the desk. Little Roberto trembled.

"You betray me. How dare you? You betray me, your colleagues, the family. We have been a family to you and this is how you treat us? This is how you repay me?"

Little Roberto's chair looked as if it was getting bigger as he sank into it with his shoulders slumped looking like he wanted to roll up into a little ball and disappear into the leather upholstery. He wondered if a response was required to his boss's questions, and even if that was the case he felt it might be unwise to even speak. He sat motionless for a while with real fear in his eyes, but knowing that in the past Capriolo's crazy outbursts would usually burn themselves out. He allowed the tirade to continue uninterrupted.

Now Capriolo came around his desk and bent to put his face within a millimeter of the object of his fury. The little man flinched as the tone lowered to the hush of a mafia boss issuing a death threat.

"You go behind my back to Nastasi. How dare you issue a formal complaint against one of us? You are nothing. You don't exist anymore."

When Capriolo walked back around his desk and sat in his chair, Little Roberto felt that this might be the safest time to try to mount some defence of his actions.

"Boss it is . . ."

That was as far as he got. Capriolo almost dived over the desk.

"Get out of my sight before I kill you. You are Judas. Now go."

Keeping his eyes firmly fixed on his boss, Little Roberto walked backwards out of the office and very gently closed the door.

In an office along the corridor, Peter Nastasi shook his head as he handed a cup of coffee to Kelly Henry and flopped into his high back leather chair.

"Roberto's walking around looking like a second rate prize fighter and the guy he puts in charge of the team whilst he sorts out the Christie situation has disappeared too. This place is gonna be like *The Marie Celeste* if this keeps up."

Kelly nodded reassuringly "It's not a PR dream that's for sure, but I get paid to handle this stuff."

"OK well go and ask him to come in here Kelly."

She flinched.

"Are you kidding? You just heard the row coming from his office. You want me to go in there?"

There was a knock at the door and Capriolo popped his head round, running his hand through his thick grey hair.

"I prepare the team for the game. Paulo, he is not in the right frame of mind now, and Little Roberto . . . well. Kelly, we have to act decisively now, sort all this thing out. Get the idiot journalist and his friend with the boots to meet me at Vincenzo's this afternoon. We see if we can bring everything to a head. Then there will be some changes."

Nastasi sat back in his chair with an air of authority.

"Changes. Yes. That's exactly what I was thinking Roberto."

CHAPTER TWENTY-SEVEN
HIPPIES OR SOMETHING

Pete, the lad rescued from the Skoda, was still a little dazed when Jonathan and Paulo led the way into the clearing that was The Hermit. His breathing seemed normal and every so often Paulo checked his pulse and gave him a look over.

Until now, his few utterances had been either tinged with bitter resentment at being stopped from carrying through his plan or simply deadpan and unemotional. He was after all someone for whom life had ceased to be something to celebrate, if indeed it ever had been.

On seeing the cave though, he suddenly became interested, almost animated and a smile spread across his face, something that he had thought could never happen again.

"You live in a cave? What are you, like hippies or something? This is well cool."

It may have been pretty basic, but as far as Pete was concerned these living arrangements were a substantial step up from his. He'd spent the previous six months living in his battered old Skoda with Paula, a seventeen year old who was pregnant when he met her. The Skoda had cost £325, which used up most of the £500 that Pete had won on a lottery scratchcard. It was old, battered and bruised, but it kept the rain off and ran reasonably well most of the time.

It wasn't meant to be forever, just until Pete could get a job and get some money together to rent a place for Paula and the baby, but getting a job was hard for a homeless young man with nothing on his CV and an address that moved from car park to car park, layby to wasteland. He'd known that the baby wasn't his. Paula was already carrying it when she was thrown out onto the streets by her so-called boyfriend Loz. It didn't bother Pete. All he had ever wanted was a family. Here was a chance to get one, to have someone to look after and care for, maybe even to have someone who cared for him, though that was an optional extra. He knew he could get by if there was just someone to care for.

They lived on takeaways much of the time, which was great at first. They'd laughed a lot and talked about a future together with the baby. But the winter had not been easy. Living in a car got harder once the novelty had worn off, but Pete had felt that if they could just get through the winter the tide would turn, he'd get a job and despite all the discomforts he was happier than he had ever been. For the first time in his life he had something to look forward to, something to make life worth living.

Then she took it away. Without warning she just upped and went back to live with Loz who promised that he'd changed. She still loved Loz she said. Always had and always would. When Pete went round to beg her to come back to the car, Loz showed that he hadn't changed that much.

Pete left battered, bruised and alone in the world. Just him and the Skoda, he had decided it was a world that he no longer wanted to be a part of. A length of garden hose and a clearing in the woods was all he needed.

Two or three more minutes and he would have been history. Free from all that life had heaped upon him. Happy he had thought, happier than even in the early days with Paula and the Skoda.

"We've got some Pontefract Cakes somewhere" said Jonathan, "Do you want some?"

Pete pulled a face "Nah. Thanks though. You got any burgers or anything like that?"

"No, but some friends are coming up later, they'll probably bring some food and stuff. Stay for a bit and make sure you're okay. We don't want you trying to top yourself again."

Pete looked indifferent, but didn't try to decline Jonathan's offer, he just wandered outside where Paulo had begun to work at the garden, using a spade that Marrielle had picked up from B&Q along with a small hand rake and a trowel. Pete went and sat on a rock and watched him carefully. There had been a small kitchen garden when he was in social care, Pete was one of the kids who would tend it, a couple of sessions a week in return for a small payment which he and the other kids mockingly called 'wages'. He'd got to know all the herbs and even got to like some of them, especially the coriander. 'The Prince of Herbs' as the gardener used to like to call it. Pete liked to put fresh, chopped coriander on his meal on curry nights and he felt it tasted all the better because, he'd watched it grow, protected it from invading weeds and most of all because he had cared for it.

"You could do with putting some manure in there mate, if you want things to grow that is. Well rotted, otherwise you'll burn the roots of the plants" Pete said.

Paulo looked indignant and leaned on his spade handle.

"You so clever? Why not you have a go?"

"Okay" said Pete, grabbing the spade and making a series of long striations on the dry soil. He began to dig a long trench about one spade deep, heaping the earth neatly to the side, creating a small hillock the length of the trench. Paulo watched, impressed with the systematic and tidy way the lad was going about his work. On reaching the end of the trench, he planted the spade in the ground and looked over to Paulo.

"Now, we could really do with some well rotted. What we do is fill the trench with the manure and then dig another trench alongside it and put the soil on top of the manure, then just keep doing that until we've got ourselves a plot. It's called double digging."

Paulo nodded appreciatively, surprised that the kid seemed to know what he was doing. Pete leaned on the shovel handle and began to wobble backwards and forwards taking deeper breaths.

"Catch him" Jonathan shouted causing Paulo to leap and

just about do enough to break the fall as Pete's body keeled over and headed earthwards. Paulo lifted the lad's thin, scrawny frame as if he was lifting a feather and carried him into the cave, covering him with a quilt on Jonathan's makeshift bed.

"Better you lie down for a bit. It was just a dizzy spell, we need to get you fed and watered before you go anywhere."

Pete felt too weak to argue, not that he had wanted to and lay cocooned in the quilt watching as Paulo headed back to the garden.

"Mate" Pete said "Er Paulo. Why are you doing this? Why are you looking after me?"

Paulo had to think for a moment and then he shrugged "Why not?" he said.

Jonathan was surveying Pete's work in the garden, walking along the trench and back again, looking at the small hillock Pete had created he ran his eye along it and smiled.

"That's got a certain beauty about it, don't you think Paulo?"

"Am I supposed to answer that one? Beauty? You are talking about a hole in the ground."

"Yeah, but the way he described it was nice. You know how you empty one trench and fill another. It's a bit like an equation, a beautiful equation. It's a bit like they do with computers, where everything's ones and zeros. The empty trenches are the zeros and then when you fill them in, the zero changes to a one and so it goes on until you have a finished plot. Do you get it?"

Paulo didn't really get it but he nodded anyway.

Silently Jonathan beckoned Paulo to come closer, paddling

his hands and nodding his head backwards, until he came within earshot.

"You remember the pencils?" he whispered to a bemused looking Paulo. "Remember what I said when we had six pencils and there were just five of us?"

"I don't know, something about another person or something?"

Holding Paulo tightly by the shoulders, Jonathan stared deeply into Paulo's eyes as if he were about to reveal something of the utmost importance.

"Exactly. I said another person was coming. It was the lad in there. That pencil was for him to rewrite his life. Don't you think that's amazing, a kid who wasn't going to have a life can now rewrite it in pencil?"

There was an intensity in Jonathan's eyes that unnerved Paulo and he pulled back from his shoulder grip.

"Is just a pencil. He is just a kid. It was coincidence, pure chance that we found him when we did. Another two minutes and we would have just found a dead body. That's all."

"Coincidence?" Jonathan laughed "That's just it Paulo. There's no such thing as coincidence. It's just the universe telling you to act."

"The universe telling you what? Where you get this shit from? No don't tell me. Halborg yes?"

"It's Halmund."

"Whatever."

Through the trees they could hear Marrielle making her now familiar high-pitched cuckoo sound. She appeared carrying two heavily laden Tesco carrier bags bought courtesy of a generous donation from Paulo, and laid them down before examining the newly dug trench.

"It's the sixth pencil Marrielle" Jonathan said as if she would immediately grasp what he was talking about. She didn't and he took her by the hand and pointed at the lad in the cave.

"Will he be all right?"

"He fine" said Paulo as if he were in charge of all matters medical "We wake him in a while, but he breathing normal so just leave him for now."

They ate some bread and cheese and Jonathan asked Paulo if he still had the map that they had been making. It took some persuasion for Paulo to take it out of his top pocket and share it, but when Jonathan suggested that they should mark the spot where Pete was found and give it a name, Paulo insisted that this was a task for him. They debated where the exact spot should be and eventually came to an agreement. Paulo drew a small amoeba type shape to represent the clearing and wrote inside it *Terra del sesto matita*. This he explained meant 'Land of the Sixth Pencil', which pleased Jonathan so much that he slapped Paulo's back and shook his hand.

They gathered around a fresh sheet of A3 paper that Jonathan had ripped from his pad, whilst he sketched out an aerial view of the garden plot that Pete had begun digging, alternately putting a one then a zero at the top of each column. Then to show how the soil from one trench fills another to make a zero into a one he placed at the bottom of the column the opposite of what was at the top, and then finished with a large looping arrow to represent the soil from the first trench being used to fill the last trench allowing him to insert the final one.

"Don't you think that's amazing Marrielle?"

"It's kind of interesting" she said politely.

"It's an equation eh Paulo? If Moonboots was here he'd understand it."

"Maybe. But he and Brian wanted to stay in the village for a while. They might come up later. You two can have fun with your little equations. Maybe we could finish the garden."

Jonathan looked closely at his lines with ones and zeros at the top and bottom then thrust the paper in front of Paulo.

"Look the ones turn the zeros from nothing into something."

Paulo wasn't sure what his reaction was meant to be, so he nodded and looked to Marrielle for some support.

"Don't you get it Paulo? I'm a one. I'm the goalkeeper. Number one that's me. I'm a one."

"Okay" said Paulo, trying to get Jonathan to back off out of his personal space "You're a one. That's good."

Jonathan stood up and towered over Paulo and Marrielle.

"Remember what we used to say a lot in the team meetings Paulo? We used to say 'football's a numbers game'. Well life's like that mate. Life's a numbers game and I'm a one."

He walked back over to the trench and began admiring it once more. Paulo looked over to Marrielle quizzically.

"He's a one" she said with a smile.

CHAPTER TWENTY-EIGHT
MORE TEACUPS

Vincenzo, it seemed, had no end of metal trays that he could continue to bang together in his back kitchen. This was not what Roberto Capriolo needed right now. He sat alone with his elbows pressed onto his usual table whilst his fingers moved up and down massaging his brow.

It was always tough at the top. He got the accolades when things went well of course, but during the course of a season there were always doubts, uncertainties and fears. His backroom team had proved good sounding boards, helping him to weigh up key decisions, but he knew that to a degree they would always go along with his view. They were not 'Yes Men', they would argue options and combinations, but not too hard. The buck stopped with him and he knew it. He'd become a master of bravado. Appearing always to be in control, always certain of his actions, yet he knew that inside he was raging with self-doubt, fighting with the fear of a humiliating downfall. It was the fear of being relegated to being a footballing nobody that got him out of bed in the mornings, much, much more than the quest for glory.

"Vincenzo" he shouted at the door to his tiny kitchen "For Heaven's sake what are you doing in there, building a battleship?"

Vincenzo emerged holding two dark brown stained baking trays as if he were about to leave to join the percussion section of The Trieste Symphony Orchestra.

"Is normal. I clean. You want something?"

Capriolo ordered a brandy, a request that was so unusual, it caused Vincenzo to pour himself a glass and take a seat with his most loyal and most loved customer.

"Roberto, you know me. Unless you ask my opinion, I don't get involved in the things you say here. It is like going to the doctors when you come here. Is confidential and I don't pry. Now for once I speak. There is something bad which is causing all this. You must take the bad bit as if it is a cancer and cut it out. Maybe you are tinkering around at the edges. I say cut it out. Bang" he rocked the table with his fist. "If it is Christie just sack him and he is gone."

Taking a sip of his brandy, Capriolo breathed deeply and pursed his lips.

"Jonathan? I don't think he is bad. Paulo, Little Roberto are they bad? I'm not happy with them, but they are not bad. Is me. If there is a cancer is me. It's all about me. Always."

Vincenzo stood up and grabbed a paper napkin from his counter and offered it to Capriolo, who mopped his tear-filled eyes.

"It is the Angel's share from the brandy Roberto, sometimes it can get up your nostrils and make your eyes water."

"Is no Angel's share Vincenzo. I am genuinely sad. I look at my behaviour often and I can always justify it. Always it is for the good of the team, the pursuit of the project. These days I begin to wonder about myself. Am I a good man?"

Mentally, Vincenzo totted up his takings since the Capriolo bandwagon had rolled into his village. His eyes widened.

"You are a good man Roberto. One of the best. Successful. You look after your boys in here. I see what you do. There is only one Roberto Capriolo."

There was a rattling at the locked door as Dugdale and Moonboots tried to gain entry. Vincenzo stood up and walked over to the door.

"We is closed" he said making his cut throat gesture.

Capriolo sighed, "Vincenzo, enough with this. You know they come to see me, let's not go through the pantomime today, I don't need it."

Silently, Vincenzo made a great play of unlocking the door as if he were cracking a safe. If he couldn't go through with the pantomime routine, he was at least going to make sure that they would have to wait. Finally he opened the door, refusing to make eye contact with the pair, simply staring upwards at some invisible spot on the ceiling. He slammed the door behind them and locked the bolts as loudly as he could.

Capriolo recovered his self-assured façade and beckoned the men to sit down. There was a renewed banging of metal trays from the back kitchen.

"Drinking already Roberto?" Dugdale said nodding towards the two empty brandy glasses.

"Is medicinal that's all. It helps to clear my sinuses."

Moonboots craned his neck in the direction of the kitchen. "I don't suppose ..."

"He come when he ready" Capriolo said sharply, "Now I tired of messing around. I want to fix everything quickly now. What do you know about Jonathan? Where he hiding?"

The pair looked at each other. Moonboots had insisted on rehearsing their answers to the range of questions that Capriolo might have asked and they were surprised that he had asked the simplest question of all. The 'route one scenario' as Moonboots had called it. The planned response was to delay.

"We know he's local" Dugdale said "We've got a source close to him. He's not looking to make any trouble for you just now, but things could change quickly."

"If your source knows where he is, get them now, phone them and bring them here. We finish it today."

Dugdale fidgeted as Moonboots moved in "She doesn't have a phone."

"Don't be stupid. Everybody has a phone. Look at me I have two phones."

"She's kind of different. A bit of a hippie type, you know, not really part of this world."

Capriolo raised his eyebrows then sat silently for a moment before reaching for a brown envelope on the chair next to him and slamming it on the table like a discarded napkin.

"You know all about brown envelopes Brian in your business. This is the proverbial 'brown envelope'. We end this thing today. Look inside."

In truth, Dugdale had talked a lot about brown envelopes

and over the years, even written the odd piece about managers taking 'bungs' but this was the first brown envelope he had ever actually seen. At least it was the first brown envelope that he had seen packed with cash. Ten crisp, neat packages of fifty pound notes, each wrapped with a thin white strip were almost bursting their way out.

"Is one hundred thousand pounds Brian. Is for no messing about. No records, no tax, you just take me to Jonathan and I do the rest. You can share it with the hippie if you want to but we do it now."

Dugdale reeled backwards in his chair.

"Shit. I mean wow. That's what a hundred grand looks like. Wow."

He handled one of the bundles running his fingers along the silky smooth pink notes, then passed it to Moonboots so that he could do the same.

"That's certainly something to think about Roberto. I know this might sound a bit cheeky, but supposing we could bring Paulo too, would that be worth two hundred grand then?"

Capriolo leapt upright in his chair and banged both fists on the table.

"What you know about Paulo? Nobody know about Paulo, only my closest allies. Who is the Judas in the camp? Little Roberto? Fredo? Ivan? Tell me who is it?"

He grabbed his brandy glass and smashed it against the wall, instinctively judging just the right angle to cause the most dramatic smash, just as he did when he was throwing teacups.

"Is a cancer. There is a cancer in the camp and it is spreading. It has to stop and it has to stop now."

"It was none of your guys" Moonboots said reassuringly "Our sources tell us that the two of them are together."

The banging in the kitchen had stopped and Vincenzo stood behind his counter with his eyebrows raised, looking at Capriolo whose face appeared to have turned to stone. He sat absolutely still for what seemed like a very long moment and then he swallowed hard.

"Together?" he whispered "What you mean together?"

Sensing another eruption, Dugdale slid the remaining brandy glass across the table so that it was out of reach of Capriolo.

"When we say together, we mean physically together . . . no that doesn't sound right, we believe that they are in the same place. Together."

"I don't understand. Why would Paulo disappear to be with one of my players who has disappeared? It makes no sense."

There was a nervous clearing of the throat from Dugdale.

"It's a bit delicate Roberto. It's early days yet and our sources are a bit confused, but, it's possible, just a possibility, that you know . . ."

Capriolo sat open mouthed. Moonboots continued.

"Yes it's possible that they're, you know . . . an 'item' as they say."

There was a glare from Capriolo in the direction of Vincenzo, who hurriedly went back into his kitchen and busied himself by banging things together.

Capriolo reached for the brown envelope and placed it back on the chair at the side of him. His hands began to shake with fury.

THE ART OF BEING ONE

"You are treading a very dangerous line here. You dare to suggest that my goalkeeper and my best friend are . . . I kill you, you pair of freaks." He stood up rocking the table and knocking the brandy glass to the floor.

Vincenzo came running out of his kitchen and ran around his counter, placing himself between Capriolo and the pair, he began jostling them towards the door. They both knew that it was time to make an exit and Dugdale rattled the locked door, becoming more frantic as Capriolo continued his tirade.

"If I ever see you two again, I swear I will rip off your heads and pour the blood in the gutter. Get out of my sight."

Vincenzo showed that if he wanted to he could unlock and open the door in double quick time, he pushed each of them and snarled as they fell into the street, before locking the door and leaning with his back against it.

Capriolo's face was bright red as he paced up and down, then there was a loud crack as he punched the plasterboard wall hard, making knuckle shaped dents in the surface and smearing it with blood and skin.

Vincenzo went behind the counter and silently handed him a teacup. No words were needed. The teacup hit the wall at just the right angle and small pieces of pottery jingle-jangled on the terracotta floor.

CHAPTER TWENTY-NINE
ONE RED PAPERCLIP

Pete sat in the passenger seat of Clementine and gave Marrielle directions to Beech Bank Farm. He knew the place well. There was a small gravel layby just down the road where he and Paula used to stay sometimes when they were moved on from the town centre car parks.

Just as he had predicted there was a sign on the drive that led up to the riding stables.

WELL-ROTTED HORSE MANURE. FREE. BRING YOUR OWN BAGS.

There was a plentiful supply. Two large hillocks matted together by straw. Thoughtfully the owners had left a pitchfork in each to encourage anyone that they could to remove as much as they possibly could. Marrielle produced a roll of black bin liners and Pete jumped out of the van and grabbed one of the pitchforks.

"I can see Clementine is going to need a good bath after moving this stuff about" said Marrielle, holding a bin liner open for Pete to scoop the first forkfuls of manure into it.

"Not really. It doesn't smell very much when its rotted and this stuff looks like it's been here for ages. The smell's in the methane gas you see, and that releases itself over time."

Marrielle was impressed "Sounds like you know a lot about . . . waste products."

"You mean shit? Yes, shit's my business Marrielle. I know a lot about shit. My whole life's been shit."

He stopped shovelling for a moment and leaned on his fork "Even with Paula, that was going to change it all. We were happy in a way living in that car. Then that turned to shit, just like everything else does. Just like this will, you watch, we'll get this garden going and then something shit will happen" he said, turning and thrusting the fork into the manure matting as if delivering a killer blow.

She looked at him wondering how such a young man who ought to have everything in front of him could be so disaffected.

"My mentor Halmund used to say 'Whenever you feel down, just concentrate all of your attention on something you love'."

Frustrated, he threw a forkful into the bag smearing Marrielle's hands with brown manure and pieces of straw.

"Yeah, well your mate Halmund's full of shit too. I hate everything about my life. Everything. Well except Mustard."

Reluctantly Pete allowed a small smile to crack the hard lines of his face.

Marrielle dropped the bag and clasped her hands together excitedly.

"Oooh you love mustard. Me too. Which do you prefer English or French?"

He chuckled. "You're funny you Marrielle. Mustard's my car. She's like a person. My best mate, my only mate."

Holding out her hand in high five fashion, she thrust it in Pete's direction.

"I'll tell you what Pete, I'll be your mate and Clementine can be Mustard's mate. How about that?"

There was a look of suspicion on his face, then he wiped his hand against his purple tracksuit bottoms and slapped his palm against Marrielle's.

"You're mad you are Marrielle" and though he tried to stop himself, he couldn't avoid letting out a giggle.

"See Pete, Halmund was right. First you smiled, now you can't stop laughing, just because you started to think about Mustard. You can't argue with it. It works every time doesn't it?"

"Maybe" he said shaking a cake of straw and manure clear of his trainers "But I'm still covered in shit aren't I?"

They managed to get eight bags into Clementine through the side door and a couple of smaller bags squeezed in through the back window, which Pete reckoned might be enough to double-dig the plot in the way that he had shown Paulo, and even if it wasn't enough there was plenty more manure to go at.

Paulo needed to be reassured that he would be allowed

to fill the first trench before he could be persuaded to walk to the road in order to transport bags of manure, but once he had committed he carried two bags and returned for two more. Pete suggested that they empty the bags onto a single pile away from the cave entrance so as not to attract insects, and as soon as this was complete Paulo set to work on filling the first trench. Pete stood by him giving words of encouragement and then a bit of advice on the best technique for rolling over the second trench onto the manure filled first trench. When Paulo reached the end of the second trench, he turned delighted to Pete and held out his hand at forty-five degrees for him to grasp.

"We doing it kid, we doing it. We are the champion double-diggers eh?"

They stayed locked hand in hand as if they had just scored a goal and Paulo orchestrated a pulsating gesture and then slapped him on the shoulder. When they moved to look at the site of the next trench, Paulo politely handed the shovel to Pete as if bestowing a great honour and the lad responded likewise. They continued the digging and filling offering each other advice whether it was welcome or not, and bantering about the quality of each other's workmanship.

Watching this from a distance Jonathan smiled encouragingly and chuckled at Paulo's competitiveness whilst doodling on his A3 pad. Marrielle slid beside him on the tree stump and ran her palm over the top of his hand.

"Drawing yourself in pencil again?" she asked.

"No" he said showing her his pad that was awash with numbers, arrows and circles and in the centre was a large black number one. "I'm trying to do that calculation that

Moonboots talked about. The Moon and back in fifty-one turns of the page. I can't get it can you?"

"I get the idea. That's enough isn't it?"

He squeezed her hand tight "I don't think it is Marrielle. I don't think that's enough. I think I'm meant to do something with it. Something big."

She laughed, "You're going to the moon and back? I like it. Well, I hope you figure it out." She kissed him gently on the lips "But you won't go anywhere without telling me will you? I know now you have a history of disappearing."

Four Tesco shopping bags were dropped into The Hermit, closely followed by Dugdale and Moonboots who appeared through the undergrowth. They were triumphant and began exhibiting the bits of food and drink that they had brought up from the village like a couple of all conquering tribal heroes.

"Who's the new lad?" Dugdale enquired.

"It's Pete" said Marrielle quietly, "He's lovely. He needs a bit of looking after so if you're coming up here be nice yes?"

"We're always nice, aren't we Moonboots? Look at all of this stuff we've just lugged up here. That's nice isn't it?" Moonboots nodded.

"Yes" said Jonathan "That's nice Brian, but we need to have a word about you coming up here don't we?"

Dugdale flushed "I'm not a journalist anymore. I quit, I told you that."

"Don't they say 'Once a journalist, always a journalist? I think you're after a story Brian. Am I right?"

There was some huffing and puffing before Dugdale looked to Moonboots for support. "Well", said Moonboots "It's like this..."

Jonathan interrupted "No Moonboots it's like this. I've got a proposition for you. For both of you. Let's go into my office" he said walking to the cave entrance "Excuse us Marrielle."

Pete had now removed his purple tracksuit top to reveal his scrawny white arms popping out of a grey T-shirt. On his left arm was a crudely etched home-made tattoo saying 'Pete and Paula' either side of a shape which roughly looked like a heart. Taking turns with the digging he and Paulo had reached trench number six and were taking a break.

"It remind me" said Paulo "Of the little farmstead that my parents had in Umbria. As kids we all had our jobs to do. I had to tend the olive trees, some of them hundreds of years old."

Pete sat on a small rock and wiped the sweat off his brow. He looked up at Paulo like a small boy looking at his teacher "Wow, that old? Where is it that place?"

"Umbria is the most beautiful part of the most beautiful country in the world. Is in Italy" Paulo said proudly.

"Hundreds of years old though? That's like ancient. I don't even know if I'm going to live to be twenty-one, never mind anything else. I should have been an olive tree."

Marrielle interrupted "Pete, you know what it is that they grow out of don't you? All that stuff that you say your life's covered in produces beautiful fruit for hundreds of years."

"What, you mean shit?" asked Pete.

"I mean shit Pete. Great things come out of it."

Pete crossed his arms and Paulo noticed his scratched ink tattoo.

"Pete, why you have my name written on your arm?" Pete looked puzzled and inspected his artwork. He'd only just had enough ink to finish the tattoo. This and the scratchy nature of his own handiwork had resulted in the final 'a' in 'Paula' looking more like an oval shape so to the untutored eye, it looked more like 'Pete' on one side of a heart and 'Paulo' on the other. His eyes filled with tears at the mere thought of Paula and Marrielle wrapped both her arms around him and held tight to him. When she finally released him, Paulo squeezed the back of his neck with his fingers as if closing the jaws of a vice and then grabbed him in a playful headlock.

"Come on fella, we finish our garden eh?"

Emerging from the cave, Moonboots began laying out paper plates and plastic cups that had been bought in the last batch of Tesco supplies. Dugdale clumsily but painstakingly pulled in a four-foot long tree stump, which he was taking great delight in making into a bar, stacking up the bottles of wine and cans of beer in neat lines, before finally declaring that the bar was open. Paulo beckoned Pete to sit with him and in turn Pete asked Marrielle to sit on his other side.

Jonathan stood up and raised his hands "Listen everybody, I just want to say something. It's funny how there were six pencils and now there are six of us here. It's like it was meant to be. We don't know how long we are going to be here – Pete, you're welcome to stay – but we're all here for different reasons. We've got to stand together. That's why I've come to an agreement with Brian and Moonboots. In return for helping with the project, they will control the press rights when this little adventure comes to an end. So relax, they're with us and they won't betray us."

"Cool" said Marrielle "We've got a project? What is it?"

"I'm not sure" Jonathan confessed, "It's something to do with the numbers."

Paulo turned to Pete "Pete, do you know how many times you would have to fold a piece of paper for its thickness to reach the moon and back?"

There was no hesitation "Yeah. Fifty-one."

Moonboots looked disappointed, deprived of his opportunity to describe the concept again, whilst Paulo playfully thumped Pete's arm in slow motion.

"Everybody knows that" Pete continued, "It's a bit like 'one red paperclip'."

All eyes turned to Moonboots for an explanation but he looked as bemused as everyone else.

"One red paperclip?" Jonathan queried.

"Yeah. Don't you remember, years back? That American guy that wanted a house, but all he had was one red paperclip, so he swapped it for a house."

There was a round of laughter but Jonathan's gaze remained on Pete until the laughter stopped.

"How can you do that? Swap a paperclip for a house, nobody would do that."

"It's just like with the paper folding, you do it in small bits, but each bit doubles. Like he swapped the paperclip for a tap or something, then say he swapped the tap for a keg of beer, then swapped that for something else. In fourteen swaps, he ended up with a house. It's the same thing, when you keep doubling things they like multiply bigger than you think."

"The lad's got a point" said Moonboots "It's the same principle. Small things make a big difference."

"So" said Jonathan, "Zeros can become ones and then off you go."

"Yes" said Moonboots, "But you're losing us a bit here with the zeros and ones thing."

Jonathan looked askance "It's obvious. It doesn't matter where you apply the principle, something has to kick it off. It's always got to start with a 'one'. I'm a 'one', I'm *the* one who has to start the thing, whatever it is. That's what the project is Marrielle. I think."

Paulo put his arm around Pete, and Marrielle slipped her arm through his so that he felt wrapped up in love for the first time in his life.

"See what you would have been missing out on Pete if, you know ... you would have been missing all of this. Jonathan Christie on the art of being one."

CHAPTER THIRTY
BUDDHA MOON

Nobody was quite sure where Moonboots was going with his story about the Buddha Moon, but he was able to hold his audience quite well. When he got onto his story about the American Bob Caputi who had built a set of elliptical dishes powerful enough to send messages which would travel two-thousand light years and which may be responded to by aliens in two thousand years time, he was beginning to stretch the limits of his credibility.

But Dugdale made sure that the wine flowed and there was a relaxed feel in The Hermit, more so than at any time before.

There was every chance that Moonboots was going to move on to another one of his bizarre stories, when Jonathan suggested that some music was just what was needed. Marrielle didn't need any persuasion to go and fetch her

Hardanger fiddle and Pete volunteered to go with her, slipping his arm through hers as they made their way through the clearing.

"Are you all those New Age Travellers like?" asked Pete as Marrielle rooted about inside Clementine.

She laughed "I suppose, in a way, that might be a good way to describe us. I guess if you asked us, we're all trying to travel to somewhere new, even if we don't know where it is yet."

She handed Pete her fiddle case and a thick stick with feathers attached to each end. He didn't know where to look first. At the beauty of the case or the bizarre feathered stick. He opted for the case and ran his palms over the well worn soft leather skin.

"Wow. Can you really play the violin?"

"It's a fiddle Pete, a special one. They call it The Hardanger. They say that when the fiddle is tuned just right and when the player is tuned just right, the sound can open the gates of heaven."

"Shit. It's lucky you weren't around when I had the hosepipe stuck through Mustard's window." He stared at the floor and was silent for a while "Or maybe you were, and this weird sort of camp you've got is heaven. Maybe Paulo and Jonathan didn't get to me in time."

She rubbed her palms up and down on his arms "They got to you in time Pete. This isn't heaven."

He stared at her blankly "It's just that I've never felt so . . . never felt . . . you know."

"Yes" she said taking the fiddle case and handing him the feathered stick.

THE ART OF BEING ONE

When they got back to The Hermit, Moonboots was still in full flow, reasoning that if aliens found a digital message from Earth in two-thousand years, it would be just the same as when we discovered hieroglyphics, which were made thousands of years ago. At first they meant nothing, but our level of intelligence had moved on to the extent that someone was able to decipher the meaning. His argument ran that somewhere there is already a superior intelligence, and they may already have the solutions to some of the problems we have today.

Paulo waved his hands about as if Moonboots was wasting his valuable time. "What does it matter to us if they don't get the message for two thousand years?

"It's all about legacy Paulo. If you buy a message from this guy, you have the legal rights to the answer if . . . when it comes back. You can leave those rights in your will to your descendants. Imagine if the answer is the cure for Aids, or ends starvation, or brings people back from the dead? Your descendants own the right to the answer."

Paulo spat out a piece of bread roll in a fit of laughter "You telling me that this guy charges for you to send message? This is just a scam. How much he charge?"

Moonboots hesitated, but with all eyes on him he couldn't avoid giving an answer "Well he wants people who will be ambassadors for the world not just any old people."

Paulo persisted "So how much for the message?"

"Well, the people who have got something important to say can probably afford it."

"Ha. So how much for this email?"

"It's not an email, the signal will still be travelling through space in two thousand years."

"I ask you three times already. How much?"

Moonboots tightened his lips and then took a breath "It's one million pounds."

Dugdale sprayed beer over his trousers whilst Paulo rolled onto his side and banged his palm on the ground trying to calm his laughter.

"A million pounds for an email?" he spluttered "The guy is a genius. Caputi, the guy is an Italian genius as well. Tell me how many customers has Mr Caputi got?"

Moonboots stood up, walked over to Dugdale's makeshift bar and pulled a can from a six-pack.

"Look if you're just going to take the piss, someone else can tell us an interesting fact or two."

Paulo wasn't letting go "Come on, you start this story so you finish it. I interested. Is simple. Mr Caputi, how many customers has he got?"

After a long swig from the can Moonboots responded.

"All right, as of now, he hasn't got any, okay, happy now? But. Whoever goes first gets the biggest exposure, imagine what a story that will be when the first message goes off. It might be the message that changes the course of history for millennia. It might be the message that saves the world."

Paulo was lapping this up "Haha, it might also be the deposit on his villa in Monte Carlo"

"You're just cynical Paulo. You know what they say 'Cynical people are just positive people who don't want to be disappointed again'. I prefer to be optimistic about it. This could be the biggest breakthrough since the theory of realtivity."

"What?" asked Paulo indignantly.

"Let's not go there eh? Dugdale interrupted wearily, before

Moonboots could get started "How about some music Marrielle?"

She opened her fiddle case and asked Pete to hold the Hardanger whilst she explained about the feathered stick. It was optional she said, the early May full moon was thought to have a spiritual significance and was a good time for new beginnings. The stick with feathers on each end was a native American Indian Talking Stick to be passed around from person to person, and only the person holding the stick was allowed to talk, there could be no interruptions, only interjections if the stick holder invited them. She suggested some music first to calm the mind followed by a talking circle.

"Anyone feel uncomfortable about it? It's optional, but it can be really good" she said enthusiastically.

Paulo looked troubled "I not so sure. What we have to say?"

"You can say whatever you feel, or if you don't want to speak, you just pass the stick to the next person, but only the person holding the stick speaks okay?"

"If I have the power of veto is okay" Paulo said shrugging his shoulders "Moonboots, I speak for you maybe and you give me a million pounds?"

Moonboots grimaced "You won't be laughing like that when a message comes back from space Paulo."

"No I be eaten by the worms."

Casting a sideways glance in the direction of Jonathan checking for a reaction Dugdale asked Marrielle if she knew The Bubble Song.

There was a plucking of fiddle strings followed by some long draws of the bow. "Of course, my parents loved Doris

Day, in our house there was always all kinds of music. Let's see, how's this?"

It was an unusual rendition, beginning first with the picking sounds unique to the Hardanger then unfolding into a mixture of long crying notes mixed with intermittent picks. Moonboots stared up at the sky and began to hum along quietly before waiting his moment and breaking into a high-pitched lilt that sounded like it had no right to come from his body.

> *I'm forever blowing bubbles,*
> *Pretty bubbles in the air,*
> *They fly so high,*
> *Nearly reach the sky,*
> *Then like my dreams,*
> *They fade and die.*
> *Fortune's always hiding,*
> *I've looked everywhere,*
> *I'm forever blowing bubbles,*
> *Pretty bubbles in the air.*

Dugdale watched Jonathan throughout, but there was no hint of an expression, he just watched the bow slide across the strings and the intricate picks of Marrielle's nimble fingers. There was silence for a moment until Paulo began to clap slowly.

"Bravo. That was beautiful" he said, which served as a signal for everyone else to clap and for Dugdale to pat Moonboots on the back.

"Now we can do the talking circle" said Marrielle holding aloft the feathered stick "Who would like to go first?"

THE ART OF BEING ONE

There was silence as everybody looked at everyone else, until Jonathan leaned forward and took the stick.

"What shall I say Marrielle?"

"Say whatever you feel. Why you're here, where you're going. Whatever."

Pensively he rolled the stick and thought for a moment. "I'm here because of two guys. Two guys who tried to abuse me."

"Wait a minute" shouted Paulo.

Marrielle grabbed Paulo's arm "No Paulo. Only the person with the stick can speak. Carry on Jonathan."

"I was going to say, I think they tried to abuse me. I was abused as a kid. Maybe it was just a flashback. I don't know, but I think it's all happened for a reason. I just want to say I'm glad you're all here with me." He was about to pass the stick to Moonboots, but pulled it back.

"The other thing. Just now when you played that song. The bubbles. That's what the crowd sang. They said I was going to fade and die. I'm not going to fade. They were forgetting something. I'm a 'one'."

Moonboots winced at Jonathan's use of the word 'one' again. He didn't want to admit it, but he was still struggling to understand what he was on about. He winced a second time when Jonathan handed the stick over to him.

He puffed out his cheeks and looked at the talking stick for a while "I think some alien will pick up a message one day, despite what Paulo thinks."

Marrielle again grabbed Paulo's arm and gave him a sideways glance before he could interrupt. Moonboots continued.

"Erm. I know loads of shit, mostly about shit, but I never

do anything with it. Well, except for consistently beating the benefits system, sometimes I might add, in swashbuckling style. But is that it? Is that all there is? I've tried not to think about it too much. Maybe I should."

When he moved to pass the stick to Dugdale, he was confronted with a half turned shoulder and a flick of the hand, as if he were trying to shoo the stick away without being noticed.

There was an outstretched hand from Marrielle who took the stick, looked up to the sky and breathed deeply.

"I want say that I'm grateful to the universe for keeping Pete here and to Paulo and Jonathan for bringing him into our lives. That's all. Brian are you ready now?"

Dugdale coughed, dropped his shoulders and sighed "Okay. Give me the stick thing." He looked down at the floor. "It's not easy. It's not easy being me. I feel like a shit. Whenever anything happens up here I just see pound signs, I just see a better story. Even now when people are talking I'm thinking of the story. It kind of makes me feel a bit, you know." He held his gaze to the floor and moved the stick in the direction of Paulo.

Paulo took the stick "I want to exercise my power of veto" he said,

then handed it to Pete.

With the expression of a frightened rabbit, Pete took the stick and looked at it before looking over to Marrielle in a silent plea for support.

"Take as long as you like Pete. There's no rush. Just say what you feel."

Paulo caught Pete's eye "Remember what I said before Pete . . .."

THE ART OF BEING ONE

He choked and swallowed hard then tried to hold back his tears.

"I wanted to die. I did. Everything's been shit, always. I was abused in a kid's home just like you Jonathan. They used to call me faggot and I used to try and hide it. Paula and the kid, even though it wasn't mine, that was gonna make me normal. Then that went shit."

Tears ran helplessly down his cheeks and he gave out three loud sobs.

Paulo gripped the back of his neck in his hand "You stop if you want. You don't have to." Marrielle lifted her finger as a gentle prod to Paulo to let him continue.

"Truth is they were right. I am. I'm a faggot. I can't help it, is that so wrong? But . . . I'm glad I didn't die . . . because just being here with you . ."

He let the stick drop to the ground and fell gratefully into Marrielle's arms. Against the sounds of muffled sobbing Paulo reached out and took the stick.

"I speak now. Jonathan know this. I'm like you Pete. I've been living a lie all of my life, and Paula wasn't the answer for you. Just as Gisa isn't for me, and she is a wonderful woman. I want to be normal. You hear that Pete I want to be normal, that means I don't want to hide anymore. I just want to be me" he looked across at Jonathan "Maybe this is what you mean by your 'one', I just want to be at one with myself."

Nobody quite knew what to do next so they all sat silently staring into space until Marrielle relit the fiddle to the sound of *Slinkombas* which lifted everyone's spirits and Moonboots stood up and attempted a clumsy jig whilst

Paulo filled six plastic cups with wine and handed them around.

This time there was spontaneous raucous applause with Moonboots making some sound that was meant to be an appreciative whooping but sounded more like a fox on heat.

"I give a toast" Paulo said holding up his plastic cup. "I toast that for all of us we have the courage to be the one we really are. Is difficult. Is like an art. I toast to the art of being one."

Jonathan took a small sip of his wine "Yes. It starts with one. Tomorrow we start the project."

CHAPTER THIRTY-ONE
THE PLAN

When Marrielle agreed to take Paulo and Pete to the garden centre to get some plants for their garden, Jonathan reminded her about the carpentry tools he had asked for. They could stop in at a B&Q on the way back.

Whilst the others were occupied, it was a good time to start work on the project with Dugdale and Moonboots, so Jonathan carefully assembled the bits that he thought he needed, though he had no real idea why he needed them. There was the pad of A3 paper and some pencils; his prized Travelcard; half a bag of Pontefract cakes; and a big number one that he had drawn on a sheet of paper and coloured in with heavy pencil strokes that made indentations on the page and gave the grey a silver-like translucence in places.

"I don't think I've done a project before" Jonathan confessed. "Well unless you count the map that me and Paulo were making. That was a kind of project but we just sort of did it at random."

Dugdale tried to reassure him "Don't worry, we were always being given assignments, projects in way. I don't think I thought about it much either, I just jumped in and used my journalistic instincts, so it's okay to be random I think."

They looked at Moonboots who was surprisingly quiet. "I'll tell you what I do shall I? When a change to the benefits system comes in, it's like a project. I have to think it through properly and then make a plan. So the first thing I do is try to be clear about my objectives. Then I look at the things I can use to move towards my objectives; then I make the plan; then I do it."

"Well" Dugdale said "We've got these liquorice circles, some paper and some pencils and a tatty out of date Travelcard for the London Underground. Where do we go from here? What's it about?"

Jonathan paced up and down along the border of what was now Paulo and Pete's garden then grabbed hold of a pencil and alongside the number one he had drawn he sketched a moon and a paperclip with an arrow pointing towards it out of a circle in which he had written "Red".

"That's the one red paper clip that Pete talked about and the folding paper thing that gets you to the moon and back. I think they are going to be important."

"Forget the bits and pieces for a minute Jonathan" Moonboots advised "Concentrate on the objective. What is 'the project' about?"

Somehow Jonathan had expected that the answer would just jump out at him, but the more he looked at his random collection of bits the harder it became to discern the objective.

"Can I make a suggestion?" Dugdale asked.

"Yes. Course. We're all in this together."

"Sometimes, when I have to write a piece, the ideas just won't come, everything's jumbled, so I just walk up and down and talk to myself. Somehow, everything unjumbles and then I'm away."

Self consciously, Jonathan started walking by the boundary of the garden and turned to Dugdale for reassurance "Like this? Just up and down like this?"

"That's it, just put one foot in front of the other. That's it, you're doing it. Now whenever you're ready, just start talking to yourself. Ask yourself, what's it all about."

At first his paces were stilted. He'd grown used to having 70,000 pairs of eyes watching his every move, but to be in the gaze of just two pairs unnerved him. He found it hard to get the first words of his soliloquy out, and then stutteringly it came.

"This project is . . . it's . . . this project is about. It's about . . . small things making a big difference. Like with the paperclip and the folding paper. It's about using that power. Starting with one and making something big. It's about changing the world really. I've been getting messages from all over the place, signs, dreams. Halmund's coming into my dreams all the time now. He tells me I'm the one. I don't know what else to say now."

Dugdale stood in front of Jonathan and held him by the arms "Okay now stop there. Think about everything you've just said. Imagine it was a story you'd just written in a newspaper. Every story needs a headline. So what would be the headline that told you in a nutshell what the story was about?"

He tried to avoid Dugdale's gaze, but there was no escaping it. Brian Dugdale had suddenly rediscovered his passion for a story, something that he thought had died long ago. There was a brightness about his eyes forcing Jonathan to stare back into them.

"The headline would be . . . Change the World: Start with One."

Dugdale kept Jonathan in his grip and spoke without turning his head "Moonboots write that down in big letters. That's the objective you were looking for."

They all sat around the piece of paper that Moonboots had written on and stared at it. Moonboots nodded gently, smiling to himself "That's great that is. It looks good doesn't it? There's just one little problem."

"What's that?" asked Jonathan.

"It's a bit like the feeding of the five thousand, only Jesus at least had five loaves and two fish. Look what we've got. How are we supposed to change the world with this pile of shit?"

"I don't think this is shit" Jonathan said, "There's something magical in all of it."

Dugdale and Moonboots turned to each other and raised their eyebrows.

"In any case" Jonathan continued, "If we need it, I can always lay my hands on thirteen million quid or thereabouts."

Dugdale and Moonboots turned to each other and raised their eyebrows even higher than before.

THE ART OF BEING ONE

The others returned to find the project group cutting up Pontefract cakes into segments. They seemed to be debating the merits of different ways of slicing the pies, and at each experimentation, Moonboots would attempt a series of calculations.

Pete and Paulo showed little interest. Instead they carried their trays of bedding plants over to the garden and excitedly began to pull little root plugs from polystyrene trays, laying them out ready for planting. They argued over which was The Prince of Herbs. Pete had always loved coriander, but Paulo insisted that basil was a staple of Italian cooking and that, he said, was the best cuisine in the world. As a compromise, they laid a couple of rows, alternating the two herbs and agreed that the two complemented each other.

Marrielle laid out the tools that Jonathan had asked for including the nail gun that he had added to the list at the last moment. Originally he had planned to do a bit of wood working using the stuff that was lying around in the forest, but now he looked at them and wondered if they were yet more bits and pieces for the plan.

Dugdale was reluctant to bring any more variables into the project just yet. "Hold on. Are we settled on seven before we go any further?"

Jonathan pondered the question for a while and began piecing together a sliced up Pontefract cake. "Yes. I like the idea of seven. Like Moonboots said it's nature's number, it feels right. We start with a one, go to a seven, then what number do we end up with Moonboots?"

Moonboots stopped calculating and ran his pencil through his hair "You'll have to give me some time. It's complicated this is. I'll have to go over it again a few times, but don't worry, it's gonna be a big number."

"Ooooh" said Marrielle "You boys like your big numbers don't you. What's it all about?"

"We'll tell you soon. First we need the calculations and then we need the plan, but I'm going to need you to get some people to come to meet us. Not here, we'll have to think of somewhere we can do it. These are people in suits, people I can trust. Will you do that?"

Paulo was holding Pete's left arm closely examining his tattoo, both were giggling quietly as if totally unaware that there was anyone else around.

"Hey fellas" shouted Jonathan "There's some Pontefract cakes here, a few of them are cut up, but we might as well eat them."

Pete came over and threw a couple of the pie slices into his mouth "These are okay, but I prefer the long strips of liquorice, they taste better."

"What?" Dugdale exclaimed laughing "But they're both the same they're both made out of liquorice. How can one taste different from another? It's like saying 'I don't like spaghetti, but that penne stuff's nice." It's the same stuff, just a different shape."

Paulo flicked Dugdale's shoulder "Hey. What you talk about? Is not all the same with the pasta. Different shapes absorb the sauce differently, so it not all taste the same. Pete is right okay."

"Yeah but" countered Dugdale "There's no sauce on liquorice is there? So there you go, I was right."

Paulo was not going to be defeated "No you is not right

smart arse. If liquorice is different shape, it hit your taste buds differently, so it tastes different. I rest my case your honour. Come on Pete we go back to garden."

Dugdale looked over to Moonboots "What's that all about?" Moonboots shrugged.

"It's about the shape" said Jonathan, "All this time we've been thinking about slicing pies into seven, but we can make any shape we want. We could take a long strip and join the ends together, you know like a wristband thing. How would that effect the equation Moonboots?"

"How many wristbands would there be?"

"Seven"

"Then it's the same set of numbers."

"Good. Let's do wristbands then

CHAPTER THIRTY-TWO
THE MEET

Pete and Paulo didn't attend the meeting that Marrielle had set up in the small, hardly used café of The Silk Museum in Macclesfield. Instead they went together to walk around the National Trust gardens at Hare Hill, that had been another one of Pete's occasional overnight stops in view of the fact that the car park was only manned by volunteers and he knew that if he got lucky, there would be no volunteer available and he could stay there overnight.

Dugdale thought the café reminded him of a band that was about when he was a kid called *Sad Café*, and in truth it was a little sad, with a smattering of people who looked like they were close on retiring from their retirement. It was Marrielle's idea. She'd spotted the place on her way to B&Q and loved the displays of screen-printed silks and the marvellous collection of buttons.

They found a quiet corner and pulled together two rough-hewn oak tables and assembled six chairs. The scraping sounds of moving furniture echoed and a couple of pensioners stopped eating their cake and turned to look.

A nervous looking woman watched from behind the counter wearing a green tabard with 'Friends of The Silk Museum' embroidered in the centre. Eventually, she approached.

"We can't discriminate against travellers, but this is a quiet place and you mustn't disturb the other customers" she said, coughing nervously.

"We're not travellers" Dugdale responded. He looked at Jonathan, then Marrielle and then at Moonboots and could see her point "Well, not in the usual sense of the word."

"Well we don't serve alcohol."

"Okay" said Dugdale belligerently.

"You can't just sit here either. You'll have to buy something, we're not a charity. Well we are actually, but . . ."

Marrielle stood up and touched her arm "That's okay, I'll get the drinks."

When a man and a woman both in expensive suits joined the group, the woman behind the counter took a keen interest in the cleanliness of all the nearby tables prompting Jonathan to ask for some privacy explaining that they were discussing a confidential matter.

With his white hair, neatly trimmed white beard and permatan, Ian Weatherspoon looked more like an ageing movie star than a solicitor. He had an easy style too, relaxed so that if he were a doctor you would say he had a good bedside manner.

Julia Pennington was moulded in the style of the new breed

of private bankers. Part model, part concierge to the rich and famous, she was more at ease in St Moritz than The Silk Museum, but her job depended on being able to attend to her clients' every whim, so she was always eager to please.

Jonathan carried out the introductions and placed on the table a sealed brown envelope on which he had written 'The Plan', which he explained was confidential and he set out the circumstances under which it could be opened. There was also a new will in there. He asked Julia to do the paper work to enable him to liquidate all of his investments so that everything could be in cash and in one account.

"But Jonathan, you'll lose a fortune. Some of those investments don't mature for years yet. I'm strongly advising you not to do that."

"We need to do it for the plan to work. I don't care if I lose some money. I hear your advice, and thanks for that, but your job is to carry out my wishes isn't it?"

"Well yes, but I don't think I can get this through, there'll be a lot of questions asked."

"Refer them to Ian. He's my representative. He'll find a way to get it through. Tell them to remember something. It's my money."

The unflappable Ian Weatherspoon had sat quietly listening and nodding with a faint smile on his face. He sat a little back from the table with his legs crossed and rubbed his beard gently.

"Jonathan, I don't know what this is all about, but it's my duty as your representative to point out a few things. Firstly, it's fine for you to make a new will, anyone can, but you do know that if there was any indication that it was made under duress" he looked one by one into the eyes of the other three "Then the will would be illegal and couldn't be carried out."

"Hold on a minute mate. What you suggesting?" Dugdale slammed his coffee cup on the table.

Weatherspoon raised his hand to continue.

"Secondly, a will is only valid if the person making it is of sound mind. I just feel that I have a duty to point those things out Jonathan that's all."

"You think I'm mad don't you?" Jonathan said.

"I'm not saying that Jonathan. Just that in view of recent events and in view of the circumstances, I would strongly advise you to seek some professional counselling."

Julia rubbed Jonathan's arm "I can arrange that Jonathan. We've got a very good guy we use, he's been on *This Morning*."

"I've got some very good people around me thanks. I'm more sane now than I've ever been. I can see things more clearly. My priorities have changed that's all. Now I've never asked either of you for much have I? You've both done very well out of me. I'm asking you to help me to do something that's important to me. More important than anything. Ian, I can change my advisor if you want. I appreciate your advice, but it's just that. Advice. I can choose whether to take it or not."

"Of course you can Jonathan" he said, calmly "I just wouldn't be doing my job if I didn't raise the issue. I can always do the paperwork you know that, but I've always looked beyond the paperwork, you know that too. Whatever this plan is, the last thing you want is to see it go wrong."

"We've been over it and over it Ian. We've looked at all the downsides, all the possible hitches, everything. All you have to do is carry out the instructions as soon as I say we are ready to press the button. You'll know when that is."

There were anxious looks between the two advisors as they prepared to leave. Jonathan looked to reassure them.

"I know how this must look. Me looking like this, doing what I've done, but just do as I ask. You won't understand just yet, but you are going to be part of something very big. It's going to be like going to the moon and back in fifty-one turns of the page."

There were quizzical looks, so he continued to try to build a persuasive argument.

"You know, like swapping a paperclip for a house. It's gonna be that amazing" he enthused, drawing a wide smile from Marrielle.

Ian Weatherspoon looked even more concerned.

"Jonathan, do you know today's date?"

It was a simple enough question, and Jonathan lent forward expecting the answer to roll off his tongue. It didn't so he sat back and tried to work backwards. The plan; Pete; the meeting with Paulo; The Hermit; Dugdale & Moonboots; the journey in Clementine; Marrielle; the forest; Reverend Darren; Upton Park Station; The match; the bubble song. It was confusing. Now he thought about it, the days had all seemed to merge into one, he couldn't be sure.

"Well I know it was a Saturday when I walked off the pitch, that's for sure"

"So you know what day it is today don't you?" Weatherspoon asked.

Jonathan looked hard at the oaken table top as if trying to read the answer in the grain.

"Actually Ian" he said raising his head "I don't know what day it is okay? But I do know that you're my paid advisor so if I want to know what day it is I can ask you can't I?"

Weatherspoon sat down again, and pulled the chair close so that he could lean forward and look directly into Jonathan's eyes.

"Jonathan. Who is the Prime Minister?"

Jonathan looked around the room anxiously and caught the eye of the lady behind the counter who gave him a stern look. He returned his gaze to Weatherspoon who remained still waiting, trying to gauge his state of mind.

"I'm not even going to justify that question with an answer Ian. Like I say, advisors can be changed. Now are you going to be the catalyst for the plan or not?"

"I'm not happy Jonathan. I'll take your instructions and I'll take your plan, but I ask you again to consider getting some counselling."

"I've had all the counselling I need mate. I'm surrounded by wisdom here. These people, me, you two, we're gonna change the world, you wait and see."

Weatherspoon and Pennington agreed to spend the afternoon setting up a liquidation plan, to switch all assets to cash and left looking more anxious than when they had arrived. The lady from behind the counter came over and started clearing empty coffee cups.

"Can I ask you a question love?" Jonathan asked.

"If you must. What is it?"

"Who is the Prime Minister?"

CHAPTER THIRTY-THREE
THE MONEY SHOT

Dugdale had come up with the idea. His view was that to get maximum media exposure for the project, they needed a striking image, a photo opportunity that could get people enthused about what they were trying to do.

Moonboots liked the idea of getting some steel tubing, bending it into the form of a giant paperclip and painting it red. He thought it would look great mounted on the edge of Stormy Point with its five hundred foot sheer drop and view across the Cheshire Plain. Everyone liked the idea, but it was true that getting the steel to bend in just the right curves so that it actually looked like a giant paperclip was a tall order way beyond their capabilities. They did like the idea of Stormy Point though, especially Jonathan.

"Yes, that's got a certain beauty to it that idea" he said, "It's kind of poetic. I like it."

They tried out various other ideas, Jonathan in the cave looking like a wild man; Jonathan standing in between Clementine and Mustard looking like a wild man; but nothing quite had the appeal of doing something that was both striking and symbolic right on the edge of Stormy Point.

"I want it also to send out a message to Capriolo and his friends Fanni and Mushi. They're the reason I'm here really. I came because they wanted to cover up something bad and what I've done is uncovered something good. It's bizarre. It's that thing again, a 'one' changes a zero, bad turns to good. That's the story we've got to get over to people."

The three of them trekked over to Stormy Point to get a better feel for the lay of the land. Dugdale climbed onto a small outcrop on a hill away to the left and made box shapes with his hands as if he were directing a movie. Marrielle's camera would be needed to get just the right shot, but this was definitely the place to do it from. When Jonathan was ready for the shot, they would need to be quick. They didn't want any random hikers or dog walkers wandering through, so it was decided that Moonboots would position himself at the gateway to the footpath and find some way of keeping them there. He was well practised at maintaining monologues in the face of disinterested strangers so he was delighted to be given this job. They even did a little rehearsal, with Jonathan shouting what they had agreed should be the codeword "Zeros to Ones." All three ran in their different directions.

THE ART OF BEING ONE

Jonathan performed his actions like a mime act, Dugdale made some more box shapes with his hands, and Moonboots talked to himself at length by the gate.

All that remained now was to get the tools and start work on the final piece of the plan, the piece that would push the button and catapult Ian Weatherspoon into action.

At first Jonathan wanted to do everything properly. He marked out mortise and tenon joints on various pieces of wood that they had collected from the forest floor, but it was slow going. The size of the joints was one thing, but nobody possessed any particular flair with a chisel. Moonboots calculated that at the rate of progress they were making the job could take up to four weeks. Dugdale suggested a short cut using the nail gun rather than precision joints, reasoning that they weren't building something to last, it was simply a piece of theatre that had to look good for the photo. These were props, nothing more. After that, work progressed quickly and they concentrated on doing the groundwork at Stormy Point. Dugdale stood on the rocky outcrop that was the intended position for the photo shot and directed Jonathan on where to dig three small holes about a foot deep.

"That's it we're ready to go" Jonathan said piling earth around the holes to use as infill.

"Right let's just do it then" said Dugdale "I'll go and get Marrielle's camera."

"No we're not ready yet"

"But you just said 'We're ready to go'. He did didn't he Moonboots?"

"Yep" Moonboots nodded "You might know who the Prime Minister is, but you did just contradict yourself there mate."

Jonathan walked to the edge of the sandstone escarpment and looked down at the drop. "Everything's in place, that's what I meant, but it's not time yet."

"When will it be time?" asked Dugdale.

"I don't know. I expect there'll be some sort of signal. Probably from Halmund"

As Dugdale rolled his eyes, Moonboots returned a supportive grimace. They looked on as Jonathan began to rummage around in his pockets, slowly at first and then becoming slightly frantic taking shallow breaths as if having a panic attack.

"My Travelcard. I've lost my Travelcard."

They looked at each other incredulously.

"It's in the envelope" Moonboots said "It's part of the plan. Remember?"

There was a look of confusion as he stared out into the far distance.

"Oh." He said looking as if he was straining to remember "Oh yes. The plan. Yes that's right, it's part of the plan. Hey we still need the shirts. Don't forget to ask Marrielle to go into town and get them."

"Right" said Dugdale, "We get the shirts and then we really are ready. Let's hope you get some sort of a signal from Halmund or whoever soon. We just need to do it, someone's going to find you soon, then we lose control, they'll write what they like, you'll end up looking like a nutter."

Dugdale agreed to find Marrielle and make the journey into town to get the shirts. They had to be just right and there was no doubt he was best placed to ensure that they were just as they should be. Jonathan and Moonboots were left with the heavy work of getting the set in place, using the three small holes they had dug and in-filling with earth and rocks that they found lying around. They were pleased with the work and went over to the photo position to admire it. Both made box shapes with their hands just as Dugdale had done and then high-fived with Moonboots letting out a whoop, but Jonathan was staring straight ahead as if trying to get his eyes to take the photo.

Four hikers came and stood on the edge of Stormy Point and looked at the set bewildered for a minute or two, and then began taking photos of each other in various poses alongside it.

"They probably think its modern art" Moonboots laughed.

"It is" Jonathan said, "I call it the art of being one." He smiled. "I like that, don't you?"

"Very good mate, but we're going to have to do it quick, once the rangers find out they'll tear it down. Any signal from Halmund yet?"

"Nothing. Maybe I should go and lie down in the cave see if I can doze a bit. He usually comes in a dream."

"He would. Why can't he just communicate like normal people? Phone, email, even fax, you know a letter, a word in the ear? Anything, we just need to get on with it."

Jonathan chuckled "Normal people? What's normal?"

CHAPTER THIRTY-FOUR
METAPHORS

Pete and Paulo sat in the summerhouse at Hare Hill, surveying a large rectangular lawn inside an ancient walled garden. They had explored the circuitous footpaths of the wild garden outside the walls, tried to name some of the plants and flowers that they came across and ran up and over the wooden humpback bridge that crossed a stream, and then did it again in the opposite direction.

They sat together in what was a comfortable silence until a small baby rabbit hopped onto the edge of the lawn. Paulo silently tiptoed towards it until he dared to go no further, then crouched and stared intently at the little creature as it nibbled on a buttercup that had emerged in between mowings.

Pete whipped around the side of Paulo and made a desperate lunge for the rabbit.

"Kill it" he said, coming a hopeless second as the rabbit

skidadled across the lawn to safety, leaving him sprawled on the grass.

Paulo looked distressed.

"Pete why you want to kill the bobtail? He no harm you."

"I don't know. It's just what you do isn't it? You see an animal and you try to kill it."

Paulo towered over Pete.

"Where you get this idea from? You want that I should kill you?"

He curled up into a ball.

"No. Don't hurt me Paulo. I'm sorry. It's just that's what we always did at the kids home. We just liked killing things."

"Stand up Pete."

Shakily he pulled himself up to his feet and cowered, holding his arms in front of his face in preparation for a beating. Instead Paulo placed his arms around him and hugged him hard.

"I no understand that Pete but I will not judge you. We need to look after all living things, not hurt them. Especially the little things. That rabbit was just a baby."

"Sorry Paulo. I've ruined it now haven't I?"

Paulo gave him a brisk slap on the back.

"You no ruin anything Pete. You make a mistake that's all. We all make mistakes."

They walked and leaned against the ancient garden wall by the archway that was the entrance to the lawn, and took in the gentle rays of the sun.

After a long silence Pete let out a contented sigh.

"It's good though Paulo isn't it?"

"What is good?"

Pete stood away from the wall and raised his hands in the air.

"All this. The garden we've been making at The Hermit."

There was nothing more than a faint nod from Paulo as he pursed his lips. Pete continued.

"Us?" He hesitated for a moment. "Us. Me and you. It's good isn't it? Me and you, we could go somewhere."

Two furrows appeared in the middle of Paulo's brow.

"We have gone somewhere. We are here at Hare Hill. That's somewhere."

"No I mean *somewhere*. We could go to Blackpool. I could get a job in an arcade or on the fair. We could have a garden. Make our own garden Paulo, me and you eh?"

There was silence and Pete placed his hand in Paulo's, which was sharply withdrawn as Paulo pushed himself away from the wall.

"What you talk about Pete? I have Gisa and the bambinos to look after. I go nowhere."

"But you said when we did the talking stick thing. You said you didn't want to live a lie anymore."

Paulo took a deep breath and nodded.

"Maybe I did. But we were drinking and the fire can have an effect. My kids. They are what is important. When they leave home then it will be time for Paulo. Right now my bambinos are like the little bobtail you tried to kill, they need someone looking after them."

"You said you wanted to be happy" Pete implored.

"Happy? What is happiness? We are men. We have to do what is right. For now it is like my gaffer say, I have to die so that others may live. We all have to make sacrifices."

The stone archway now framed Paulo and he gave a mock salute. Pete fell to his knees.

"I don't get it Paulo"

"It is a metaphor Pete. Take care pal."

He turned and began to jog along a rough path towards the road. Pete sank even further and a tear shot along his cheek and formed a dark spot on his maroon shell suit.

"I hate metaphors. Metaphors are shit."

CHAPTER THIRTY-FIVE
SO THAT OTHERS MAY LIVE

It was unusual to say the least for a football manager to cycle, let alone cycle into work. For Roberto Capriolo it kept him in touch with a passion that otherwise he would have little time for, it also gave him forty-five minutes of thinking time, a chance to unravel whatever problems he might have to deal with, to experiment in his mind with different tactics, to go over his appraisal of the dangers of whoever the next opposition team were going to be. Often he would lose himself in deep thought in the saddle to the point where on some days when he sat in his office and reflected, he could remember nothing of the journey to work. He cycled in on a kind of autopilot setting.

This day he had more to think about than ever. With the season at a critical stage all he wanted was calm and focus, but it was hard even for him to focus. Irving Friedel, the owner, had taken the unusual step of flying in for a meeting instead of video conferencing and would be arriving late in the afternoon. It was, he was told, to be a crunch meeting. That sounded ominous, especially as Friedel had issued a press statement a day earlier expressing a 'vote of confidence' in the manager and his handling of the Christie situation. Votes of confidence tended to be the kiss of death in the cutthroat world of football management everybody knew that.

Capriolo knew as he cycled across the traffic lights in Wilmslow that his thoughts should be on the team, but he found it hard to stop his mind from wandering. Was this it? Was this the end? Total humiliation despite all he had achieved. He pictured himself sitting in the stands at some match or other on a wet Wednesday in November, surrounded by a bunch of other washed up former managers, like vultures waiting for the slow painful death of whichever manager was going through a bad patch.

He jumped the lights without thinking and had to brake hard, narrowly avoiding going over the handlebars as the orange VW Camper pulled out in front of him and screeched to a halt in the middle of the junction.

"You" he shouted to Dugdale who was sitting in the passenger seat "You're a total liability. You and this hippie-mobile. You could have killed me."

Dugdale signaled to Marrielle to drive on rapidly. She hesitated "Shouldn't we get out and see if he's okay?"

"Nah. There was no contact. Drive on, looks like he's getting aggressive." He signaled again whirling his hand like a spin dryer.

There was a renewed sense of urgency now. It had seemed to take an age for the kid in the shop to press the transfers onto the shirts. All Dugdale wanted to do now was get the photo, kick off the plan and sell the story and image rights, but it was all taking too long, it was only a matter of time before the whole thing came crashing down. He resolved that regardless of any signal from Halmund he was determined to get Jonathan to do the photo shoot right away.

They pulled into the layby in front of Mustard. The driver's side door was open, but Pete was nowhere to be seen. Dugdale slammed the door. "The kid's trying to get someone to nick it. Probably wants to claim on the insurance. That should be worth forty-five quid at least. Bring the camera. Let's get this done and get out of here."

Jonathan heard their voices as they approached the clearing and came out of the cave entrance.

"Any word from Halmund yet?" Dugdale shouted.

"Nothing. No sign, no signal, we'll just have to wait."

"Jonathan look, we're going to get rumbled, I can feel it. Journalist's intuition if you like. It's now or never, here's the shirts you asked for, let's just do it."

"Not without a sign" he said.

Marrielle's eyes lifted to the tree canopy and her body tensed. "Jonathan look behind you" she said in a trancelike state.

A green plastic hose hung down from the branch of a nearby oak looped and knotted around Pete's neck, who hung pale, skinny and limp only a few feet off the ground. A line of dark blood the colour of his tracksuit trickled from his mouth. Frantically they cut him down and lay him on the ground. What little life there had been in Pete had trickled away. Marrielle pulled off a scrawled note that he had pinned to his purple tracksuit.

EVERYTHING ALWAYS TURNS TO SHIT. ENJOY YOUR LIFE WITH YOUR MISSUS PAULO.

Kneeling by the body Jonathan ran his hands through his hair and rocked backwards and forwards.

"This is all my fault. Paulo was here because of me. I'm responsible."

"You can't blame yourself" Marrielle said, "You and Paulo saved him."

"It's me. I started all of this stuff, now I can't finish it."

Dugdale shot Marrielle an anxious glance "Look, we're going to have to get the police. It's over, in an hour this place will be crawling with paparazzi. Why don't we just go and get the shot now while we can?"

"You're right Brian it's over . . ."

There was a commotion in the woods. Two voices shouting, one staccato. Capriolo appeared in the clearing in his white lycra and cycle helmet, being pulled and prodded by Moonboots. Before he could say anything Jonathan grabbed the shirts and reached for the nail gun "Zeros to Ones" he shouted and dived into the undergrowth in the direction of Stormy Point. Dugdale followed camera in hand to try to make it to his vantage point in time, whilst Moonboots tangled with Capriolo trying to buy some time to make the money shot.

One large wooden cross stood in between two smaller ones as close to the edge of the precipice as they could get.

Jonathan whipped the two shirts over the smaller crosses so that the backs of them were exposed to the camera. Iron-on letters ran across the top of the shirts, one "Fanni' the other 'Mushi'. Standing on the tree stump step at the base of the larger cross he leaned his back against it and stretched out his left arm, firing several shots of nails into his palm, screaming and watching the blood drip onto the dry earthen floor.

Dugdale dripped with sweat as he took up his position "Jonathan" he shouted "What have you done? Where was that in the plan?" Steeling himself he prepared to take the money shot.

"Brian" Jonathan shouted screaming with pain "I can't nail my other hand. Come over I need you to nail the other hand. I'm finished here. It's over."

A breathless Capriolo appeared with Moonboots hopelessly trying to keep up. He stood in front of the cross and looked at the shirts and removed his cycling helmet and threw it to the floor.

"Jonathan. There is no need for this. I come here for you. You come down we make everything smooth. We look after you."

"Yes? Like you looked after me before. When you wanted me to stay schtum so that these two could carry on scoring for you?" he nodded in the direction of the Fanni and Mushi shirts on perched on their little crosses.

"Look after me? Like when you asked me to die so that others may live. Well now I want you to do something for me."

He threw down the nail gun so that it fell at Capriolo's feet.

"Come up here and shoot some nails in my other hand, then just leave me to die. You asked me to do something for you, now you do something for me."

Capriolo stepped over the nail gun.

"Jonathan you are stressed. Emotional. You misunderstand my words. Is just a metaphor. We make everything right. I help you."

He climbed up onto the tree stump step and began to pull at the nails in Jonathan's left hand. Screaming in agony Jonathan instinctively headlocked the Italian with his free hand.

There was a short frantic struggle, then a sharp cracking noise echoed across the ancient sandstone landscape and bounced through a boulder strewn hillside to the flat plain below. The feebly constructed wooden cross, followed the line of sound, crashing into the abyss with the two men locked together.

Dugdale got the money shot.

Moonboots looked over The Edge and let out an unearthly wail.

Marrielle played *Bjorgumspel* sweeter than she had ever played it before.

CHAPTER THIRTY-SIX
DOUBLE BUBBLE

On the first day of the new season, on a beautiful August afternoon, Bjorn Bjørgum, at just eighteen years old, the world's youngest top-flight goalkeeper, ran onto the pitch and headed towards the home fans. He turned his back to them and wagged his thumbs over his shoulders pointing to the lettering on his shirt 'CHRISTIE 1' it said. On his wrist he wore seven mustard coloured wristbands.

There was a wave of applause, then a moment of hush until a small boy probably no more than nine years old let out a shout from the front row "One Jonathan Christie, there's only one Jonathan Christie." People closest to him, began to join in the chant lifting the musical tonality, which spread like a ripple around the stadium until it echoed through the rafters and seemed to swirl in the sky.

Bjorn Bjørgum pulled the Christie shirt over his head,

trotted over to the boy and handed him the shirt. The boy was wearing seven orange coloured bands. He took the shirt with thanks, removed a wristband and swapped it for one of the goalkeeper's mustard coloured ones. Young Bjørgum applauded the boy and ambled back to take his position in the pre-match line up. The boy stood up and beckoned to an elderly man with a flat cap some three rows back. He handed him the shirt and in return the old man swapped a green wristband for an orange one.

A goodwill epidemic had begun.

Some months earlier, Ian Weatherspoon had opened the envelope marked 'The Plan' in the presence of Dugdale and Moonboots as he had been instructed. It had been expected that Jonathan Christie would have been present too, but his revised will meant that the plan could be enacted with or without him.

Some years earlier when the German goalkeeper had committed suicide, Jonathan had given a newspaper interview on the loneliness of being a goalkeeper. He had been paid two-thousand pounds, but felt bad about accepting it in view of the circumstances, so Weatherspoon had set up a not-for-profit company 'The One Foundation' to receive it. He was the Company Secretary and Jonathan the Director. The idea was that when Jonathan finished his playing career he could pick this up and do something with it, so it was just left there doing nothing.

As Weatherspoon began to unfold The Plan, all of Jonathan's assets were transferred to The One Foundation as he had requested. Moonboots, or as he now wished to be known Brian 'Moonboots' O'Reilly was appointed Director of Operations and Brian Dugdale became Director of Communications.

Their first job was to address an envelope to a church in the East End of London. Some days later Reverend Darren opened the envelope. There wasn't much there. He pulled out a ten-pound note which had been folded over several times into a small package. When he opened it there was a London Underground one-day Travelcard with a tear stained letter 'T' forming the shape of a cross. A message was scrawled on it in Jonathan's handwriting 'Compound interest on one good deed', and stapled to it was a cheque for one million and one pounds.

They ordered seven million sets of coloured wristbands, each with a GPS tag stamped inside it. Over one million were placed on the seats of football stadia, the rest were given away through supermarkets and schools. It was a simple system. People were encouraged to perform a small act of self-sacrifice for someone else and when this happened wrist bands were exchanged. Anyone who was able to collect one wristband of each colour could send them into The One Foundation with a suggestion of what to do with the prize money. The prize was one million and one pounds and the winner would be the person who came up with the self-sacrifice that was a small thing that made the biggest difference.

Brian 'Moonboots' O'Reilly had done the calculations when they had been up at The Hermit. If seven million people perform seven acts of kindness it would result in a epidemic of goodwill so big, it would make going to the moon and back in fifty-one turns of the page seem pretty insignificant. Even allowing for the fact that some people will drop off and not complete the seven and some people will cheat and try to get the seven coloured bands by other means, he concluded that it was still a very, very big number. At first they were worried about the cheats, but as Jonathan had pointed out, if you cheat all that you get is the chance to make a bigger self sacrifice by finding a way to make one million and one pounds help others.

After Bjorn Bjørgum made the first wrist band swap, Dugdale and Moonboots signed over to The One Foundation the image rights to their precious money shot of Jonathan and Capriolo going over the edge together. In return Ian Weatherspoon exchanged a wristband with both of them. When a wave of goodwill spread across the country, Hollywood celebrities began sporting the bands and soon the trend spread to New York. After that doing good things for other people became an unstoppable force.

Brian 'Moonboots' O'Reilly had commissioned geographers at The University of Manchester to track the GPS patterns of the wristbands and after the first year, produced a huge World Map of Goodwill showing how the movement had spread, and tracking the movement of the Christie shirt. It stopped in a small settlement outside of Saskatchewan.

The National Geographical Society paid one million and one pounds for the framed version of the map.

"He'd have liked that" said Moonboots.

"Yeah. He would" Dugdale replied as they sealed and posted one more envelope.

Moe *Stordhal had a reputation in the Narvic Bar & Grill. He was excitable and emotional and people had got used to it, but even the regulars had to admit that they had never seen Moe in such a state.*

He trembled as he sat and beheld Marrielle and Halmund Bjørgum, together, master and pupil, sitting there in front of him in the Narvic Bar & Grill of all places.

Eric placed a shot of Aquavit in front of him, and he shakily but hastily gulped it down and slammed the glass hard on the table staring open mouthed as Marrielle and Halmund tuned their fiddles.

The tuning subsided, there was a silence and then the room filled to the mysterious sound of Bjorgumspel played in a harmony the like of which had not been heard before. A strange fog appeared around an empty bar stool and as the fog gently lifted a bearded man in a Transport for London hi-vis jacket became visible as Halmund reached a crescendo.

The whole of Narvic rocked with applause, the banging of tables and the stamping of feet.

"Friends" Halmund cried out "Please welcome Christiana's newest resident. I give you Mr Jonathan Christie. He was always my Number One."

Eric leaned across the bar and shook Jonathan's hand.

"Welcome to Narvic Bar & Grill Jonathan. Can I get you a beer?"

"I don't really . . . yeah why not?"

"You're better off here Jonathan than in the outer world. That place is doomed."

"Hmmm" Jonathan rubbed his beard "I'm not so sure."

"Ha" Eric said wiping the counter and placing a glass of beer on a Narvic coaster "I wouldn't put money on it."

"No?" Jonathan took a sip from the glass and breathed a sigh "I did."

On the terrace of a white walled villa in the hills high above Monte Carlo, Bob Caputi poured himself a glass of Dom Perignon and set it down by his computer.

He opened an envelope and prepared to send his first message. A message that he said would travel into space for two thousand years. He typed it very carefully using one finger, checked it again for accuracy, took a deep breath and pressed the send button. It read -

'I AM ONE. WHO ARE YOU? JONATHAN CHRISTIE'.

Raising his glass of champagne he looked out to the azure sky.

"Salut, Mr Jonathan Christie, whoever you are, wherever you are."

THE ART OF BEING ONE

He placed the glass down on a heavy marble coffee table and looked for a moment as if he was waiting for a reply.

Just then a single bubble rose to the top of the glass. It pushed against the surface.

And then.

The bubble.

Burst.

ABOUT THE AUTHOR

Malcolm McClean's first book *Bearhunt: Earn your living by doing what you love* was translated into Turkish, Chinese, Korean, Romanian and a special version was produced for the Indian market. He subsequently published *To the Edge: Entrepeneurial secrets*, before a successful foray into ghost-writing. He wrote *Thinking Outside the Box* with Brad Friedel and the Sunday Times Best Seller *The Didi Man: My love affair with Liverpool* with Dietmar Hamann.

He continues to enjoy a career in business where he is the founder of Bearhunt; The It's a Goal! Foundation; and The School of Curiosity.

He lives in Alderley Edge.